❧ *Pool of Blood* ☙

<u>Fiction Series</u>

The Alex Evercrest Series
The River Front
The Girl on The Grill
Missing
Maggot
Racist
Votive Candles
Windy City
Country Road
Pool of Blood
Sins of the Daughter
Body Parts
The Skull Collector
The Vanishing
The Shadow Fighter
Moonshine
Grief's Trajectory
The Magic Touch
Northern Lights
Alex Evercrest Heroine
Alex Evercrest Collection Two
New Direction
A Family Affair
Disruption
The St. Lebuinnus Church Murder

A Brian O'Neil Novel
Hawaiian Phoenix
Moon Curser
Death Broker

The Problem Solver Series
Solutions
Drug Lords
Border Crosser
The Problem Solver Collection

<u>The Taelo Series</u>
Taelo: The Early Years
Taelo: The Golden Feather
Taelo: Journey of Discovery
Taelo: Dangerous Passage
Taelo: Condor Clan Slingers
Taelo: Circumvention
Taelo: The Journey of Sages
Taelo: Collection
Taelo: Future Leaders Journey

<u>A Taelo Story:</u>
White Swan and Quiet Pheasant
The Child's Name
Floating Cloud
Quiet Rabbit
Busy Bee
Little Otter & Talking Wren
Broken Spear
Burley Bear & Meadow Flower
Taelo Story Collection

<u>Science Fiction</u>

The Savitar Series:
Journey's End
Savitar
Confluence
Savitar Series Collection

Bram Nielson Series
The Fold
The Message
Fold Wormhole
Negative Fold
Ripples in Time
Bram Nielson Collection

<u>Single Science Fiction Books:</u>
Current Past and Future
The Event
The Door
Viajante 7

ഇ Pool of Blood രു
By: *Ron Mueller*

Around the World Publishing LLC
Cincinnati, Ohio

ISBN 13: 978-1-68223-343-6

Distributed by Ingram
Alex Evercrest Model By: Pi03@ShutterStock
Cincinnati Scene: Nagel Photography @ShutterStock
Cover Design By: Ron Mueller

Dedicated to the people of Hawaii.

<u>Pool of Blood</u>

<u>1 Revenge</u>

The pressure of Mason's foot kept Okani's head in the toilet. He was sure he was going to drown. Then Mason grabbed him by the belt and threw him out of the stall and kicked him in the side and shouted that if Okani ever looked at his girl again, he would not only beat him to a pulp but would carve up his face so that he would look just like the joker in the Batman movie. Okani stayed on the floor until Mason left the bathroom.

Okani woke up in a cold sweat. This was a nightmare that he often had about his high school years. Mason had made his life hell then and to this day he often relived those hell moments at night.

He wished that it would have been different. He wished he would have been more of a fighter, but there was no going back and changing things. He had done nothing wrong then and he could not change what had happened.

He had to deal with what was the now.

He made coffee, sat down with a piece of buttered toast and thought about his current life.

He felt good about this current stage in his life.

He had his own house. Yes, he had to make monthly payments to the holder of his deed, but he was the "owner." He had made various improvements to his property and home that included putting in a new cement driveway trimmed with red brick.

He had laid a new brick patio with a fire pit and purchased a canvass cover that had a large opening over the fire pit. He was proud of his yard in which he had planted various flowering plants. He was proud to have one of the best-looking yards in the neighborhood.

And inside, he had built an inset display case, that ran the length of the living room. A panoramic photo of the two-stream waterfall and pool that he now thought of as his special place was mounted on a special frame operated by three pistons that would push the picture up to show the contents in the display case.

The left stream was snow white and the right stream was a light red hue. He had edited the picture to put in the red hue. The red hue symbolized blood flowing into the pool below. He was extremely proud at his handiwork.

The beauty of it all was that he could sit in his recliner and use a remote control to open the display case for viewing.

The hidden display case project had taken him almost a year to complete but now as he sat in his black recliner with his feet raised and pressed the button, he could enjoy his knife collection with the surge of pride that welled through his body.

Each knife had a special meaning to him. Each knife was smaller than the previous one. Each knife had a picture under it and below each picture there was a memory stick hanging on a thin delicate silver chain.

Life was good.

He knew that he was living the good life.

He felt that he had made it.

He had overcome his mother constantly telling him that he would never amount to anything. And he was overjoyed that his father, who had often beaten him, had been silenced by a heart attack during one of his drunken moments. They were both in a different world and he hoped that his father was in hell.

He now felt that he was powerful and in command of his life. He had a good job and made additional money as a bartender.

What really made his life good was that he had achieved his life's ambition to repay his tormentor for the years of humiliation and mental torture that he had experienced.

He had vowed to get even but for what seemed like a lifetime, the right time or situation never materialized. And even worse, for that whole time, he had no idea of what the get even follow through action of revenge would be.

The memory of his high school years remained and was often a part of the nightmares that he often experienced.

He knew that those memories would haunt him until he went to his grave.

He felt blessed that he had the epiphany that gave him the vision of how to repay is tormentor.

The epiphany had hit him when he had stopped to swim in a pool, on the road to Hanna. There were two water streams cascading from the rocks above. He marveled at the grace that the water had as it fell and hit the smooth surface of the rocks at the edge of the pool below.

He absorbed the sound of the water and the mist in the air and felt his whole body relax.

He climbed up to the top of the falls and looked down into the crystal clear water below. He jumped and sank to the bottom and then he pushed off to get back to the surface. He repeated the jump several times.

He found a path that was an easier way to the top. He was walking up the path when suddenly the idea of swimming in a pool of blood hit him.

He knew that the blood he wanted to swim in was that of his high school tormentor, Mason.

He shouted out in a loud voice and raced the rest of the way up to the top and the jumped into the pool below. He stayed at the bottom of the pool until he had to push up or drown.

He let out a loud shout as he surfaced. He had been given the vision for which he had prayed.

In his enlightened state, it was hard for him to drive back to his house.

His focus from that day forward had been in figuring out how he would be able to get Mason to the falls. He wanted be able to control the situation and make Mason understand what was going to happen.

He wanted him to suffer and be afraid.

He wanted Mason to feel desperate like he had felt when Mason had put his foot on the back of his head and held it in the toilet.

He wanted to see the fear in Mason's eyes and to see the life leave Mason's body.

Drugging Mason was the solution that seemed the most realistic. How to be around him to drug him at the right time became the challenge.

He used social media to locate Mason and learn where he lived. He followed Mason and learned where he went drinking. It turned out that Mason had a standing Thursday night out with some friends at a local bar.

It took Okani a few months more before he was able to get a bar tenders job at that bar. His heart always beat faster when he went to work on Thursday evenings which was the day that Mason would show up to drink with his friends.

In one conversation he heard Mason boasting that he always walked to the bar so that he could drink as much as he wanted.

A few weeks later it thrilled Okani as he watched his adversary celebrate a pay increase and drink a little more than usual.

He decided that this would be the night. He had been prepared for this night for weeks. Now all he had to do was to get Mason to leave in a state that he could control.

He slipped some ecstasy into Mason's last drink and then checked out from work.

The excitement was hard for him to control.

He had been prepared for this moment for several weeks.

He was ready. He was prepared.

He followed a very drunk Mason to his house where he offered to help him. Mason welcomed him and let him guide him.

He was able to guide Mason into his car and drive away. Mason passed out in the passenger seat.

Okani took his time driving the road to Hanna. He knew that his biggest challenge would be to get Mason back to consciousness.

Mason was at least fifty pounds heavier than he was. He did not want to carry Mason to the top of the falls.

He turned on the radio and tuned into his favorite station.

When he got to the falls, he parked his car well into the brush and made sure that it was not visible from the road.

He then carried the basket that he had designed, built, and tested, that would hold Mason's body as he bled to death and put it into position at the top the right-hand water stream. He set up his camera tripod and made sure that he had everything arranged the way he wanted.

He hoped that the moon light was good enough for a good picture. He had the camera on video mode. He had set up his camera to be controlled by his phone.

Then he went down and guided the still very drunk and drugged Mason and guided him up the slope to the top.

There he undressed him and struggled to get him into the basket. He shackled Mason's ankles to the basket's wire mess and hand cuffed his hands behind his back.

Mason was slowly coming around.

The cold water and some of the strongest coffee that Okani could make, brought, Mason slowly back into the awake world.

Okani waited for a while just looking at Mason and enjoying the moment.

He finally asked him if he knew who was standing in front of him.

That seemed to bring Mason into an awake state, and he rudely replied that the queer from high school who looked just as ugly now as then, was standing in front of him.

Okani delivered a resounding backhand to Mason and then taped his mouth shut. He did not want Mason to be able to scream out during the next part of what was about to happen to him.

Mason immediately started to struggle. The look on his face and his wide eyes when he saw the almost foot long bowie knife thrilled Okani.

He nicked Mason across various parts of his body.

He laughed and mimicked the scene from a movie that had the acter laughing through a crazy smile saying, "I'm back," but he said, "It's payback time and you won't like the payback."

He felt lightheaded and he could feel his heart pounding. He enjoyed the moment and the rush it was producing. He knew that taking his time was worth every moment.

He reminded Mason of all the times that he had slammed him into the lockers or had pushed him from behind, the time he had forced his face into the food that was on his tray at lunch and finally he reminded him of the time he had pushed his face into the toilet.

After each reminder, he flicked his knife and made a small cut on Mason's chest. He again was thrilled by the look of alarm in Mason's eyes. He watched as Mason seemed to be saying he was sorry or maybe pleading for Okani to stop.

He would have loved to be able to hear Mason plead and scream, but he could not chance someone hearing the screams.

Okani mimicked Mason's voice and said, "Oh are your sorry now?"

He made several additional cuts on Mason's chest and stomach.

He was thrilled by the small streams of blood slowly trickling down Mason's body. Each blood stream seemed to be finding a different path to the water below.

The vision of the water falling pink over the falls filled his head.

Mason fell to his knees as he struggled to get away.

Okani stepped into the basket so that he could lift Mason back to his feet.

Mason at first resisted but the knife placed under his chin convinced him to stand. Once he was up Okani pushed the knife in about an inch and smiled as Mason tried to lift his head upward.

That was when Okani let him know that time had run out and that he Okani would swim in the pool below with Mason's blood flowing down from up above.

Mason was wildly shaking his head and trying to shout.

Okani quietly said that he was enjoying the payback and that it was extra sweet, but it needed a salty follow through.

He leaned in and looked Mason directly in his eyes as he made the first cut on the left neck vein. Then he did the same with the right vein.

He laughed as he saw fear in Mason's face and watched the light begin to fade in his eyes before he crumpled into the basket and the water flowed over him.

The moment that the blood, squirting out from the slashed neck veins hit Okani's tongue, a brilliant, bright flash imprinted his brain with the salty taste of heaven.

Okani stood on edge of the flat stone above the pool and jumped into the pool below.

He looked up and was disappointed that there was not enough blood to turn the water red. The right stream flow with a slightly pink color for a few moments as he swam in the pool looking up to where the basket holding Mason was located.

He swam around the pool several time and then he returned to the top.

He carried Mason's body up stream to a crevasse that he had found. There he rolled Mason down into the crack in the stone crevasse and made sure he was tightly wedged in.

Then he spread a generous layer of lye over him and then poured several bags of kitty litter to absorb the odor of decay.

Finally, he covered the body with several layers of stone.

He looked at his handy work and he threw a dead pine tree and some leaves on the stones. He decided that it looked like it had been that way for a long time.

He returned everything to his car and climbed one last time to the top of the falls and after making sure everything was pristine, he jumped into the clear water in the pool below.

He came out of the crystal-clear water feeling refreshed and he felt that life had just gotten significantly better.

He returned to his car feeling more alive than he had ever felt.

During the day he continued to work at the Hardware store and in the evenings, he worked part-time at the bar.

It was at least two months later when he heard the drinking group that Mason had been a part of talking about the fact that no one had seen or heard from him. They wondered where he had gone.

Okani smiled because he knew, and he served himself a shot of the best Courvoisier that he had. Just the thought of that night warmed his heart the Courvoisier warmed his throat and stomach.

He knew that life was good.

He kept close track of the local news and continued to monitor the conversations of the drinking group.

The local news never had a report on any missing person and the drinking group never talked about Mason again.

A year seemed to flash by.

He was sitting in his recliner with a glass of wine. He pressed play and his favorite video came up on his huge, curved theater television screen. The music that he had dubbed in began and the scene of the water fall with the full moon providing the ghostly lighting, the rushing water hitting the pool below provided the ephemeral setting for the clip that he had edited to enhance it and in the video the water ran pink the entire time. But it was the futile struggling of his lifelong antagonist that provided the substance and enhanced the visual sweetness that always caused starbursts in his mind.

The anguish and the look of fear was the sweet icing on the cake.

It was a dream come true.

The only word that made any sense to Okani to describe that moment was ecstasy, or rapture or maybe bliss. He decided that all three words were true.

He continued to watch his favorite video. He had watched this video showing the point in his life, where it had taken the upward path, many times.

It was the most important moment of his life.

He was the star and director of the scenes that, as they flashed on the screen caused him to catch his breath and to hear the sound of his beating heart.

Then came a day when he once again wished for the rush that he had felt when he cut Mason's throat and tasted his blood.

He craved another experience like the first one.

He knew the old saying, "the water flows under the bridge but once," or was the saying he wanted, "there is only one first time."

He decided that it didn't matter and that he was going to see if he could get close to that same feeling again.

He wondered how he was going to find his next swim partner. He looked through his High School yearbook and picked out several potential candidates. He identified a mix of men and women. He was not sure how to pick any specific one. The ones he picked all deserved to be in his basket.

Several months went by, when by chance a woman came into the hardware store where he was working as a checkout clerk.

She was looking for a specific brand of stain remover and cleaner. After she got what she wanted and a few other items, she came to check out with a variety of goods and asked to pay by check.

Okani had recognized her immediately, but it was clear to him that she did not know him though she had been a groupie in the group that Mason had more or less been the leader of, and she was one of the loudest voices repeating what Mason was saying to harass him.

She had been two years behind him.

He followed the store's procedure for someone wanting to pay by check and asked for her ID. She gave him her driver's license. He scanned her license and knew that he had all the information he needed to track her down.

Later after she left, he printed out the information. Lilanni Aleman, age 29, address 415 Lacunna drive.

She became the focus of who would be his second swim partner.

He spent more than a month monitoring her small older home and found out that she lived alone. She seemed to spend much of her time at work and then in the evening watching TV. It seemed that she did not have many friends and only went out periodically

He knew whose blood he would swim in next. He began to imagine how the swim would make him feel.

He wondered whether he should have sex with her but decided it was too messy, and he was not into that to begin with.

He wondered if the taste of her blood would be different from that which he remembered from Mason.

When the full moon arrived, he made his move. He was able to overpower her at her house and take her to the falls with her hands wire-tied behind her and her mouth taped shut.

On the way he reminded her about all the times she had participated in harassing him. He could tell that she was trying to say she was sorry.

"I'm so sorry," Okani said in his version of a feminine voice.

He took his time driving to the falls. Once there he put the basket and the camera in place before leading her up the path to the top of the waterfall. He found that she was easy to put in the basket. He chained her ankles to the bottom of the basket.

He then stripped her naked.

That had her screaming behind her taped mouth, and her eyes were as large a saucers.

The tears streaming down her cheeks gave him the high that he had been hoping for.

The fear in her eyes took him up high.

Tears running down both cheeks took him higher.

He knew that this was as good of a boost as when he was doing Mason.

He had replaced the bowie knife with a long thin bladed carving knife used to slice prosciutto. It had thin blade that had a feminine beauty.

He flicked the knife and made three small cuts across her chest and then watched the blood run across her breasts and down along her stomach.

He bent down and licked the stream going between her breasts and then licked a tear off her cheek.

Her blood tasted different, it seemed sweeter, and the salty tear seemed to balance the taste experience.

It reminded him of the wine tasting that he had done at the local wine stand that catered to tourists.

He laughed at the connection that his mind had made.

He quietly told her that he was going to slowly cut nicks along her entire body until the blood provided her with a red coat that looked like a lace see through lingerie.

He looked her in the eyes and the shaking of her head made his pulse increase. He knew that the feeling he was experiencing was better than sex.

He then looked into her eyes and slowly slashed her throat and opened his mouth.

Yes! Salty but much better tasting than Mason's blood. He let the sputtering blood cover his face as he watched the life begin to leave her eyes. He lowered her into position in the basket and then jumped into the pool below.

He knew that he was crazy, but he also felt more alive than he had ever been.

He was crazy in love with his new life and the power that he felt when he went for a swim in a pool of blood.

He knew that this was what he wanted.

He thought about how he needed to manage holding on to this new life. He decided that he wanted to get a better day job and that he would rotate his evening job as a bar tender around the various bars so that he would be able to identify his next swimming partner.

2 Missing Persons

*T*he Maui Detective unit was a small three-person operation that was a part of the larger statewide Hawaii Police Department.

It had a reputation for successfully solving its assignments.

All the personnel in the department were born in Hawaii and mixed well with the local population.

Leilani Dickens, the current supervisor of the unit was from the big Island of Hawaii and on her way to Oahu at her next promotion.

She was keen to solve a big case that would make that happen or would put her in the position to make that move.

She kept her eye on the prize and worked hard to make sure she was on the promotion platform.

Her two field detectives, Malia Aukai and David Kalama were rather young but good detectives that had been delivering good results, but she knew that she needed some sort of great result.

She needed it but they were on a small island and getting a big case was not currently in sight.

To say she was not thrilled, when the local Chief of Police, basically her boss on Maui, asked her to take on a case dealing with missing persons that had stumped the people normally handling that issue, was a huge understatement.

She had tried but had failed to deflect the request and was told straight forward that the Chief was asking politely but the only answer was for her to say yes.

She said she understood and quietly said she would take the case.

David hung up his phone, looked over at Malia and asked if she was up to finding missing persons.

She responded by asking when detectives had started to follow up on missing persons.

David replied since their boss had assigned them to that task. He let Malia know that they were being called to come to her office and get some more information.

He speculated that there was something unique about the situation otherwise they would not get involved but he then gave a small laugh and reminded Malia about her last argument with Leilani and that perhaps this was payback time.

Malia gave a small laugh and replied that it had not been an argument just a detailed discussion about getting better assignments. Assignments that would stand out when it came time for raises and promotion.

She had only reminded the boss that there were several islands that had law enforcement on them, and it took successful cases to move on to higher positions.

David said that he agreed and that was true for all of them.

She went on and said that she had heard rumors about a string of missing persons, no bodies, and no set pattern to indicate anything other than random occurrences. She wondered what had changed.

David nodded and said he had heard the same rumors as well and now the two of them would be finding out all the details and join the crowd of those complaining about the lack of any leads.

They went into their boss's office and took the chairs she waved to.

She handed each of them a request form that officially requested help from the detective unit and she pointed to a box labeled evidence. She then explained that the Chief of Police had requested their help in solving a long and growing list of missing persons.

She explained that for just over a year the list had suddenly taken an unexplained uptick and was now clicking along at a once per month clip.

Missing person's thought it might be more than some random change and might be the work of a serial killer. She went on to say this was the big case that Malia had been so adamant about getting assigned to.

She pointed out that the three of them had just been put on the point of a needle and they would either solve the case, or they would have that needle go through all of them and kill their careers.

Malia smiled and said that she had been requesting assignments that led to raises and promotions, not assignments that would have them jumping off Black Rock to drown themselves. She waved the request form and said that there was nothing there that seemed like a lead.

David looked over the request then briefly looked into the evidence box. He looked at Malia and said that there didn't seem to be much evidence in the box either.

Leilani agreed and said that she hoped the two of them could find the breakthrough that would solve the case otherwise they would all be working at some checkout counter trying to make a living.

She went on to explain that she had been ordered to take on the case and if they had to jump off of the Black Rock to drown themselves she would join in. She gave a small laugh saying that if they didn't solve this case they would all be looking for a good hotel to play security guards for or a good restaurant to become the waiters and waitresses for.

Malia laughed and quoted the old saying, "be careful what you wish for, the wish may come true." I wished for a breakthrough case but perhaps someone above heard me say a case to break Malia.

Malia picked up the box and carried it out to her desk that was situated so that she faced David.

David took the missing person report Malia handed him as she took another and said that they should begin by reading each of the reports and listing the names and addresses on the white board.

By late afternoon they were looking at the list on the board and other than the fact that all but one address was on Maui there was not a pattern in the addresses. It seemed rather a very random one that covered the island.

David suggested adding an occupation column that they then filled in. It seemed to be mostly on the service industry side with a few office and clerking positions, but it did not add any clarity. Since Maui catered to tourists and was loaded with restaurants and hotels, it was expected that many of the missing would be in the service industry.

They added an age column and got nothing more than the fact that the missing were between the ages of nineteen and thirty one.

David speculated that these would be low key targets that would not have the adamant support of the folks putting in the missing person's reports.

They added additional columns for education, and heritage and filled them in. Afterwards they stood looking at the board and Malia summed it up by saying, "There is nothing there that gives us a hint at what is going on." She went on to say that she didn't even get the feeling of it being a serial killer at work.

David suggested that they reinterview everyone who had reported the person missing and go out in the field and look at businesses around where the missing person worked to see if that would give them any additional insights.

Malia suggested they also try to learn the habits of the missing person.

David looked at the list and said they would be busy for at least the next month.

Malia agreed and suggested that they call up each person who had entered a missing person's report and set up an interview schedule.

David said he agreed but he then said that they should first talk with each of the officers who had worked the missing person case first to see what they might have learned something that was not in the report. He felt that would give them a chance to think about what more or what they could do differently to get some new insight.

Malia nodded and commented that he had just added another week to their month long work.

They were no farther ahead after the first week, but at least it had been an easy one since they met each of the officers in the office or at one of the satellite offices.

Every officer they reviewed the missing person's report with said the same thing, "good luck, and do you have your resume out looking for another job."

Or they gave their condolences and let them know that being assigned to street patrol was really not such a bad assignment.

David commented that the odds of them solving the case was ten to one against them.

After a week, the only change on the white board was the fact that they added the picture of each individual that had put in a missing person's report to it. They had no other insight or any new information.

The pictures did not give them any more understanding. The gender split seemed close to even, the looks of the people varied and did not seem to set a pattern. The fact that the age range went from early twenties to the early thirties did not seem to be critical. That was the normal age range for most service industry workers on the island. Both of them had worked in restaurants and knew that there was always the single older waiter or waitress that had worked for the restaurant forever who was more or less the manager of all of them.

It was late Friday afternoon when David threw up his hands and said that he was done for the week and that he was going to ride his bike around the Island on the weekend to see if maybe the gorgeous sights would provide a new idea on how to pursue the case.

Malia commented she was going shopping, and her family was having a picnic in the park where she would eat grilled chicken and drink some beer.

She then planned to take a long walk along the beach in hopes that some idea would come to mind. She said that jumping from the Black Rock was becoming a more inviting option than working on the white board.

The following Monday morning, over a cup of coffee, they confessed to each other that nothing had given them any new insight.

Malia pointed at the board and suggested they map out the addresses and go look at the area where each of the missing persons lived.

They looked at the pins in the map and concluded that location was not a factor. They dutifully drove to each location to get a better feeling for the missing person.

On returning to the office, David said that it was time to set up interviews with the people putting in the missing person reports.

They began the cycle of visiting the location where the missing person had lived, where they worked and then talking with the person who had put in the missing person's report.

They tried to get new information by asking about the missing person's personal life, their eating habits, their partying habits, eating out habits, their hobbies.

If they got something that was not in the report for that person they followed through to see if they could add new information to the board.

Each day they returned to their white board and checked off three people, but no new breakthrough information surfaced.

David commented that the interviewing and the new information was bringing the missing people to life for him but commented that they were not getting any breakthroughs.

Malia agreed and said that she prayed every night for a breakthrough but so far the highest detective, who knew all, had not shared anything with her. She said that she was speaking slowly and clearly so that she would not be misunderstood.

The month ended and they were no closer to solving any of the cases than when they had started.

They joked that they needed to get their resume's out.

They set up a meeting with Leilani to let her know that they were coming up empty handed.

Leilani listened to what Malia and David had done to date. When they were through she said that she was going to see if she could get the help of a detective that seemed to always solve her case.

She said that she had recently attended a nationwide convention of detectives that had been held in Cincinnati and that she had come home with a video that highlighted the Cincinnati Detective unit and had a piece on the detective she had in mind.

She asked them to sit down while she shared with them the clip that she had purchased at the convention and that highlighted a group of Cincinnati detectives who claimed to always solve their case.

The office was silent as they all watched the video clip.

The clip ended with the scene of Alex Evercrest pointing her finger out to those watching and saying, "Each of you get up each morning and go out to protect your community. Be proud, Be strong, Be excellent at what you do. Remember to treat others as you wish to be treated but get the job done."

It seemed to hit David in the head, and he just said, "Ouch."

He looked at Leilani and commented that he bet this Evercrest would do no better than he and Malia in solving their current case.

Malia jumped up at the end of the clip and in a loud and an almost shouting voice said that she had seen Alex out on Ulua beach.

She pointed back at the screen and in a loud voice declared that "Alex Evercrest is on Maui. They had to find her and challenge her to solve the missing persons cases."

Leilani gave a laughed and said that if that was indeed true, then she would personally escort the two of them to meet Alex and see if she could convince Alex to take on the case.

Leilani picked up the phone and a called over to the customs office and asked for the hotel or condo that an Alex Evercrest was staying.

She was told that she would have her answer soon, but it had to be looked up.

She was not surprised that it took almost the whole day before she got the address of the beach side house where a Ms. Evercrest was staying.

She suggested the three of them drive over to the house early the following day to see if they could meet with Alex.

The next morning, they drove out to where the house was situated right on the black lava rock on the edge of the sea.

When they got to the single lane road on the black lava rock at the edge of the ocean they knew that there were only a few very exclusive homes ahead of them.

They arrived at the address, and they all agreed that it was a secluded and very beautiful home.

Malia wondered how much such a house cost to rent and how a detective could afford to rent it.

David pointed out that there was no car in the drive on the other side of the locked gate. He speculated that Alex had already taken off on some site seeing venture. He suggested they ask if the customs office would have Alex's phone number.

Malia commented on the fact that Alex had a wonderful view of Molokini Crater and Kaho'olawe island.

She again wondered how a detective could afford to rent such a home. She looked over to Leilani and suggested that her detectives should be getting a similar salary as Alex.

Leilani countered with the fact that Malia and her partner would have to solve as many and as complex cases as Alex had.

David suggested they try calling Alex. He asked when Alex had arrived at the Island.

Leilani called her contact at the customs office and learned that Alex had arrived almost two weeks ago. She also got the phone number where she could be reached.

David suggested that Leilani call and set up a lunch meeting with Alex at a place where they could sit outdoors and away from the crowd.

He wondered if they should suggest a food truck near where Alex's house was located. He knew of two of them. One of them was always across from the park and they could get a table in the park.

Leilani said that she preferred something more upscale and would ask Alex where she preferred to meet.

She checked to make sure that her phone would identify her as an officer of the local law before she dialed. She knew that she personally ignored calls that she could not identify. She held her breath and put up her fingers showing the good luck sign.

After the fourth ring she was going to hang up when a pleasant voice answered and asked how she might be of service. That surprised Leilani and it took her a moment to focus back on getting Alex to meet with her.

After a brief discussion Leilani got Alex's agreement to meet. She was pleased to hear Alex saying that she would see what she might be able to contribute. She then agreed to a nine o'clock breakfast at a Bar and Grill that Alex said she wanted to try.

Leilani took down the address on South Kihei road.

She then hung up. She had a broad smile and said that she would treat her two detectives to breakfast at nine and gave the name of the restaurant.

She was personally wondering what this Alex person was like. Someone as successful as she was might have gotten to feel superior and might be impossible to bring into a lowly missing person's investigation.

Malia said that she had eaten lunch at the restaurant but never breakfast. She commented that she was excited about meeting Alex and hoped that the three of them could convince her to help with the missing person's case.

David said he hoped so too but wondered if there was any hope for a breakthrough in their case. He said that he was not sure what additional rock could be turned over that he and Malia had not already turned over.

He said he was looking forward to at least enjoying breakfast but did not expect much more.

Little did he know that Alex did not randomly turn over rocks in hopes of finding a worm.

She followed logic and evidence that would lead her to the solution that she envisioned and planned for.

3 Maui Escape

After the Slate cases went to court and his team's involvement was no longer needed, the Chief insisted that his four detectives take vacation.

He had been participating in the therapy sessions that they were all in, and he realized that all of them were at their psychological limit. He felt responsible for having kept them pursuing the case until the end even after having been warned by the departments phycologist.

Now he wanted his two top detective teams to recover and get refreshed so they could continue the great work they always delivered.

He let them know that he would not assign any cases to them until they all took a solid two week vacation. He pointed out that every one of them had accrued more than thirty days and Bill could take a whole quarter off and still have thirty days' vacation left.

Alex decided that a true vacation, other than going home would do her good. She talked it over with her mother who asked her what vacation that she had been on that she thought was the best one that she had taken when she was young.

Alex immediately answered that it was their trip to Hawaii. She immediately realized that Hawaii was her first choice for a vacation!

The wonderful memories she had from going there with her parents had been the substance that had often carried her through her rough times.

She thanked her mother and said that she would send post cards.

Her mother said that nowadays, daily photos could be sent via instant messaging.

Alex laughed and promised daily photos.

She talked it over with Matt.

He said that the location was a great destination. He reminded her that he did not have as much vacation accrued as she had but he would take as much time off as she desired.

She shared her previous experiences of visiting, Maui, Kauai, Oahu, and the big Island of Hawaii with her parents, and let him know the highlights of each island.

She then let him know that she wanted to keep her vacation relaxing and did not want to do any island hopping and preferred to stay for at least two weeks in Maui. She said that Maui had been the island she had enjoyed the most.

Matt was in total agreement. It would be his first time to Hawaii and if he liked it they could try some of the other locations later.

He laughed and reminder her that her last case had started with relaxation in mind and had end in her total exhaustion.

Alex nodded and agreed that so far she seemed to have been a magnet that attracted unusual cases with unusual twists.

Matt nodded his agreement and laughed as he reminded her that an attack by a helicopter gunship out in the middle of Lake Michigan, an AR-15 attack by an insane prejudiced supremist, and almost hitting a woman fleeing for her life from a band of SLATE members constituted being a magnet for the unusual.

Alex gave him a hug and said that they should try out Maui and see if they could create the memories for their old age, which was not connected to some crime that he was always talking about.

He agreed and said that he would have memories of all of what they had experienced together but this time they should focus on making peaceful and heart felt memories that were made of love.

Later she talked with Trey about what he was planning for his vacation and found out that he was going with Lindsey and Nolan to Cancun to a resort that featured a water sport experience off of a ship designed with water slides, jet skis, snorkeling, and some other water sports.

He shared that Nolan was really excited.

And he personally was looking forward to having a vacation that was not associated with their detective field work.

She and Matt flew from Atlanta non-stop to Maui and arrived early in the morning after an almost ten hour flight.

Alex suggested that they start with breakfast at a small local restaurant she had found online. After breakfast, they drove across the island to their beachside house that she had splurged on.

The road to the house reduced to a single black topped lane that ran along the black lava studded shore that the waves were crashing across.

Alex smiled as Matt reacted to the grandeur, the salty smell of seaweed and the sounds of the waves. This was the grandeur she often envisioned as she slowly went to sleep at night.

She had taken an online tour of the inside and outside of the house and had fallen in love with it. She had looked at many others but decided to splurge on this house with the excuse that she was going on vacation to recover.

The house had a six foot high stone wall fence on three sides with the black volcanic rock and the sea along the ocean side. The yard was rather small, but filled with a mix of banana trees, plum and fig trees with passion fruit trying to conquer all of them that gave it the feel of a tropical forest.

She noted immediately that it was the right time of the year since the fruit on the trees were ripe and the passion fruit had turned purple.

She had driven in so that Matt could take in the coastline.

When they arrived at the house, she pressed the opener to open the black metal eight foot high spear tipped security gates and drove in. She drove to where the laned ended and turned off the bright red Jaguar she was driving.

She smiled when she thought about her car rental. She had her own black Jaguar parked in her parents garage and would have loved to have it on the island. When she was looking for cars to rent and found the red Jaguar for rent she had immediately rented it.

Matt led the way up the walk. The entrance was through a veranda that went all the way around the house.

They both stopped to admire the stunning front door that was a black hardwood with a variety of embedded seashells and starfish sealed in clear plastic and were back lit. To say it was stunning would have been understating the effect it had on a person that was seeing it for the first time.

Alex ran her hand across the smooth black wood surface and absorbed the sensation.

The door opened into a grand room that had surrounding floor to ceiling windows looking out into the ocean and that took up the entire first floor. The screened veranda had the screens up to allow for an unobstructed view of the ocean.

She and Matt stood holding each other for a few moments as they took in the scene.

She was not planning to do much cooking, but she went to the kitchen situated at the back right corner of the grand room and stood at the cooking island that allowed a person using the gas stove to take in the ocean view. She noted that all the kitchen appliances were top of the line stainless steel with black handles. She focused on the top quality expresso/coffee maker that was well beyond what she was used to. She read the simplified instructions and felt a sense of relief. It was clear to her on how to make a cup of coffee.

Matt called her from the second floor.

She went up the stairs that went up behind the kitchen area. She stopped and stood looking out of the glass walls that had a two hundred seventy degree panoramic view of the ocean.

She walked out to the large deck where Matt was standing at a black iron rail with a big smile on his face.

He gave her a hug and said that they didn't have to go anywhere on the island but could just enjoy the house and the view and that it would be a memory they would always remember.

He complemented her on immediately creating great memories.

Alex decided that if she could figure out how to buy the house she would do so.

Alex looked back into the room and for the first time saw the king sized bed with thin white veil netting held up by four tall posts.

She took Matt's hand and said they needed to see how firm the mattress might be.

Later after changing into her swimsuit, she led the way around the yard and tried a couple of figs and passion fruit.   Afterwards she led the way to a crevasse that widened as it went out to the ocean. The crevasse had a fine sand that provided smooth walking out to where she could begin to swim.

She swam out to where the crevasse ended. From there she could see Molokini and a group of boats that were anchored there.

Matt had followed her and the two of them relaxed and floated bobbing up and down with the rhythm of the waves.

After some time, they decided to return to the house and see about lunch.

Once back in the house they took a shower to rinse off and then they selected a restaurant with outside seating and went out for a late lunch.

During lunch Alex described the various sites that she wanted to take in and she also discussed what food, snacks, and kind of coffee they should buy to take back to the house.

Matt said that his role was backup, and he would support any ground activities she desired.

She smiled and reminded him that they were on a vacation and not an assignment.

He nodded and said that starting out and watching the sunrise from Mount Haleakala sounded like the right beginning.

The drive to Hanna should be the second event.

The drive around Kahakuloa the third.

A hike on the Boy Scout trail next.

Finally, they should do the Io Valley hike.

He suggested they put a swim or rest day between each touring day.

He added that they had the most astounding place to stay that he could imagine with a private beach that was enchanting and staying in every other day seemed special. He said that he probably could stay just at the house and be satisfied.

Alex agreed but that she was going to make sure they got a full Maui experience and said that she would put together a list of places to eat during each outing and on the rest days. She added that she did not plan to do any cooking. She said that on the between days, they should plan either a late lunch or dinner and also a quick dip out in their private swim area.

After lunch they went and picked up a variety of snacks, a set of snorkels, fins, and masks for each of them and some basic food items that included eggs, coffee, bagels, and a variety of fruit.

Matt looked at all the food and commented that they would have to do a lot of swimming and hiking, or they would gain weight from the food they had just bought.

Alex agreed and said she would add a two mile run out along the lava fields to their to do list.

The next morning, Matt drove up to the top of Mount Haleakala and Alex half slept while at the same time sipping on her coffee.

Once they parked, Alex carried a blanket and a small box with a bear claw to eat while she continued sipping her coffee. She selected the same spot where she had sat when she was twelve but this time she had her soul mate with her and knew it was a memory that she would cherish.

She wrapped the blanket around them both and split the bear claw with Matt.

The sun, like a blazing nymph, rose slowly out of the sea. It was as glorious as she had remembered. This time she knew it was even better because she had someone to share her pleasure with.

It made the sunrise spectacular.

Matt gave her a hug and a kiss on the forehead and quietly said that he would remember this sunrise for a lifetime, and he would remind her of its beauty for that long.

Alex chose to drive on the way down.

Matt had said he was going to take his turn napping but was soon holding on for what he loudly proclaimed was "for dear life."

Alex laughed and when she came to the trail that led to the bottom of Haleakala volcano, she stopped and said that once they returned from going into the base, he could drive the rest of the way down.

Matt was less aggressive in his driving, but it still felt challenging to him.

Alex joked that he should quit driving so slow and that they only had few days of vacation and they needed to get down the mountain on the same day on which they had watched the sunrise.

Once they were down, she suggested they have brunch and guided Matt to a Vietnamese restaurant and ordered two bánh mì sandwiches, and some Vietnamese iced coffee.

Matt commented that the coffee had a rich, flavorful, sweet taste that he really enjoyed. He added that the sandwich was a first for him and he liked it much better than most other sandwiches.

He asked how Alex knew about this kind of food.

She reminded him that he had met her college friend, Caia Leu, now living in Augusta who had introduced her to many Vietnamese dishes.

They returned to their home rental and decided to go snorkeling.

Matt got to the end of the crevasse and then put on his mask and goggles and almost immediately began pointed down into the water.

Alex looked down and saw that there were three turtles going along the black lava rock eating the moss and seaweed growing from it.

She watched as one of the turtles surface for a moment seemed to look at the two of them and then went back down and resumed eating.

A Moray eel caught her attention and she pointed it out to Matt. She considered them one of the uglier sea creatures and they always seemed threatening.

She realized that many of her nefarious characters in her nightmares often had moray eel features.

The two of them spent the next hour snorkeling and taking turns pointing out coral and many of the colorful fish that were all around.

They were both floating and sharing what a great snorkeling location they were at when two sail boarders whizzed by. The boarders were controlling the wind chutes by pulling on the handles to move them in the direction they wanted to go. It seemed to be a thrilling way to propel across the surface of the sea.

Alex commented during dinner that she doubted that they could become proficient at doing the sail boarding they had witnessed but she was going to look up where the two of them could take a few lessons and go sail surfing. She felt that they had a chance in mastering that quickly enough to enjoy it.

Matt agreed that they should do something like that first and see if they had the balance and strength for that and then try sail boarding sometime in the future.

Alex agreed and said that she watched folks sail surfing at a beach that was on the road to Hanna, and they could combine the two and make it a really full day.

Matt suggested dinner at an Italian restaurant that boasted a view of the sea and the best Italian food on the Island.

Alex wondered how many Italian restaurants Maui had and if the best had any competition.

The restaurant located on the foot of Mt Haleakala had a huge outside deck with a view of the sea. They chose a table by the edge of the deck closest to the sea.

The waitress shared the specials. One of the specials was Frutti Di Mare.

When Alex said she was going for that special, Matt smiled and asked if she was going to eat any red meat while on vacation.

Alex replied that she was going to eat the best item at any restaurant they went to and Frutti Di Mare was it for this restaurant. She commented that the clams, mussels, scallops, and sweet succulent shrimp mixed with spaghetti sounded great. She verified that there was no wine sauce in the recipe when she placed her order.

She had ordered caffè latte so that she could enjoy it with the warm Italian bread with butter that was brought to the table.

Matte commented, to the waitress, that he was a poor boy from the country and needed education on eating Italian food and ordered exactly what she was having.

The waitress laughed and commented that the Caffe Latte was usually a breakfast drink but there was no problem getting one.

They looked out to the ocean and Matt pointed out the surfboards whizzing directly out to sea and then zig-zagging back in toward the shore and then repeating the cycle.

He commented at the speed that the boarders seemed to achieve.

Alex said that it looked like the same beach she remembered from her childhood. She asked the waitress about the beach and if a person could get some training to do surfboard sailing.

A few moments later, the waitress brought back two business cards and said that these were cards left by two different guys that rented sail surf boards.

Alex called the number on the top card. The first opening for lessons and board rental was two days out. She then called the number on the second card and found out that there was an opening early the next day due to a cancellation. Alex booked that opening and asked if there was any special requirements other than showing up. She learned that she would have to sign a standard liability exclusion waiver as part of getting lessons and going out on her own on the sail board.

She knew that such disclaimers were standard and agreed to the session.

The latte and buttered bread would have been enough to satisfy Alex but the aroma of the Frutti Di Mare had a magical effect, and she began to consume clams and mussels, between bites of seasoned spaghetti and shrimp.

After the first few bites she stopped and asked Matt what he thought of the meal.

Matt looked around and commented that the view of the ocean was second only to the food at the best Italian restaurant on the island.

That put a smile on her face and again she wondered how many Italian restaurants there were on the Island. She googled the question and found out that there were thirty five restaurants that claimed to be Italian.

Matt gave a small laugh and complemented her on picking the top one.

Once back at their house, Alex suggested a run along the road through the lava field before they settled in for the evening. She was enjoying eating what she wanted but she did not want to be putting those meals on her body.

Early the next morning they drove to Ho ʻokipa where they met their surfboard sail instructor. He took a quick measure of each of their heights and asked their weight and then led them to their boards and had them pull them away from the rest and go down the beach.

He had a board of his own and took it out into the water, where he demonstrated how to get on the board and then engage the sail. He took a quick spin out and then returned.

He then demonstrated how to get back on the board after falling off.

He had each of them get on the board and get their balance several times and then he had them get on and engage the sail.

Alex engaged her sail and immediately shot out and bounced over the first several waves before losing her balance.

She looked around and saw that Matt was still close to shore and seemed to be having difficulty.

She got back on and engaged the sail and again shot straight out away from shore. She decided to try changing direction and then turning and zig-zagging back toward the shore.

She saw Matt coming straight toward her and maneuvered out of his way.

She turned and followed behind him and soon caught up but stayed well away from him. He turned and began a zig-zag back toward the shore and she followed.

They made several runs and then together they went into the beach area where they were congratulated by their instructor.

He commented that they were one of the fast learners and said if they wanted to return he had openings two days out.

Alex said that she doubted they would be able to make it but would call if they decided to try it again. She said he would get a call in the future for sure.

Alex said that she had a great time, and that the feeling was similar to riding a fast motorcycle but without the noise.

It was still early, and Alex suggested they take the road to Hanna and go to one of the cafes that featured an ocean view and outdoor dining. She said that she was ready for breakfast.

They drove for about an hour and reached the Huelo area where they stopped and had breakfast and enjoyed the view of the ocean off Kapukaamaui Point.

Matt commented that he would need to buy a map of Maui just to remember the names of the places they were seeing. He commented that he also needed someone to pronounce some of the names, so he had some idea of how to say them.

After some coffee and some banana bread they drove on.

Alex was driving when Matt pointed to a sign declaring they were halfway to Hanna and that it declared the original banana bread originated there.

She declared that the banana bread she had eaten had tasted great.

They stopped at every water fall and took a few photos and then drove on until they were ready for lunch.

The sign pointing to the Black Sand beach changed their mind about lunch and they went there first to walk the beach which was really not sand but small black lava that required one to wear shoes.

Alex decided on just walking and staying dry.

They then drove on to Hana.

Once there they decided to eat a lunch before visiting the seven falls.

Alex ordered Edamame, and Crispy Calamari after agreeing with Matt that they would share his fourteen ounce grilled ribeye, and they would also share a Kula green salad.

Matt commented that the local beef was tasty and the blue cheese with it made it superb.

Alex agreed and added that she was enjoying the calamari with blue cheese as well. It gave the calamari a unique taste.

After lunch they went and climbed the trail to the top fall and swam in the pool below it. They worked their way down until they were back where they began.

Alex said that it was time for them to continue their drive.

The second part of their drive was the Desert Yang, to the Tropical Yin. Or as she put it, Maui was a Yin-Yang island in the middle of the pacific.

Matt commented that it was amazing that a small island would have such a contrast in environment.

The ocean view was still amazing, but the vegetation was minimal, and life seemed sparse.

The road turned away from the ocean.

It was late afternoon. They had both taken turns in driving. They were out of the area they call the desert when they came to a sign declaring the location was a Honeybee Sanctuary.

They stopped and Alex pointed out to the ocean and made the comment that they were only five miles from their house rental but would need to drive another twenty five or more miles to get there because there were no roads down the mountain to the Wailea Makena area.

They contemplated dinner at on one of the eastern area restaurants but decided to go to a restaurant in the Wailea-Makena area.

They chose to go to a restaurant with an ocean view where she ordered oysters on the half shell as an appetizer, a classic Caesar salad and Blackened Ahi as the main.

Matt ordered BBQ Pork Ribs. He said he would be the meat and potato guy and she could be the sea nymph that dined on seafood.

They both had an iced tea and then for desert they had three scoops of sorbet: passion fruit, mango, and lemon.

They asked for small plates and they shared the food that came to the table.

She was determined to stay in shape and suggested that they go home, change into their running clothes, and jog several miles out into the lava fields.

During the run they discussed the activities for the following day and agreed that it was a day to snorkel from their private access to the sea and then relax and just chill.

That evening they discovered the awesome sound system that was part of the television and other electronics that filled the shelves. They enjoyed listening to their favorite musicians and relaxing and doing some reading.

Alex commented that she was feeling much closer to her normal self and said that Maui was having the rejuvenation effect that she had hoped for.

After enjoying doing nothing and staying in for a day, they went around Kahakuloa Mountain. They had breakfast in Kahului, but it turned out to be a late lunch on the other side of the mountains when they got to Kapalua.

There they decided to eat at a Japanese Seafood restaurant. They shared a laugh when they looked at the menu that boldly featured more steak than the sushi that had attracted them.

Afterwards they decided to walk out to Makaluapuna point and get some pictures of the beach and the sea. Matt stopped at the sign with the name of the point on it and slowly pronounced it.

Alex complemented him on his Hawaiian accent.

She then suggested doing a little shopping in Lahaina. There they found several brand name retail outlet stores where she bought a blouse and a hat with a heart and the word Maui across the front.

She suggested that Matt buy a nice shirt and a hat of his choice. He went for a hat similar to hers but had the word Hawaii on it.

When they were driving the road toward their rental they stopped at a Mexican food truck and bought several shrimp, steak, chorizo, and fish tacos. She ordered a Passion fruit and Mango ice cone and Matt bought a coconut, Guava ice cone.

Once home, they took their food and ice cones out to the veranda and leisurely enjoyed watching the slowly dropping to the sea on the far horizon.

They both agreed that it had been a long day but one that they had enjoyed.

Matt said that he was going to enjoy just floating out of the point in front of the house and doing nothing the next day.

Alex said that she was looking forward to eating at Humuhumunukunukuapua'a restaurant just because of its name and said that she was looking forward to him using his fluent Hawaiian to tell her how to pronounce it.

She added that she was leaning toward their rack of lamb and that there was a great menu variety to choose from.

She added that it was going to be hard to choose from all the desert choices. She pointed out that they were surrounded by lava and the restaurant featured a dark chocolate ganache under its Lava Cake desert heading.

Matt commented that they would have to climb to the top of the mountain on the Boy Scout trail the day after just to use up all the calories that they were accumulating.

Alex agreed and said that maybe they should jog both up the trail and then back down.

Matt laughed and said that she could jog up and he would just hike up and when she came jogging back down the trail he would join her on a down the mountain jog.

Alex smiled and knew that her Hawaii vacation choice had been the right one. It got her away from the world of the crime and killing that had become her norm.

Little did she know that the world of crime was widespread and would find her even as she tried hard to escape it in the land of paradise.

4 Magnetic Attraction

*H*ow wrong Alex's conclusion about having escaped the magnetic attraction of bizarre, abnormal, criminal behavior.

It would soon breech the surface of her fantasy like a whale breaching the surface of the ocean and giving a resounding slap with its tail to emphasize how wrong she could be.

She did not know that Johnnie's diligent narrative of her many accomplishments had preceded her to Maui.

She was unaware that the Chief's video highlighting the accomplishments of his detective personnel had permeated many of the state and local law enforcement organizations.

The success of Johnnie's creation of her pointing out into the audience and saying, "Each of you get up each morning and go out to protect your community. Be proud, Be strong, Be excellent at what you do. Remember to treat others as you wish to be treated, but get the bad guy," would put her in the spotlight.

That and the fact that the Chief, like a matador waving the red flag at the bull, had also claimed that the detectives he was highlighting had solved every case they had been assigned. He had attracted the interest of many police organizations. And none more than a desperate Maui detective.

She and Matt took a break from touring because they added jogging all the beaches on Maui as one of their goals. They joked with each other that it was the only way they would keep from gaining fifty pounds from eating so well and so much.

Swimming and snorkeling off their private lava spit proved to be a great way to relax and enjoy themselves, but it did little to get them in top physical shape.

Alex felt the weight that her last case had put on her slowly lifting, and she knew that she was creating the positive memories with Matt that she desired and that would last them a lifetime.

When they had jogged the majority of the beaches, they were down to two days left on their vacation. They decided it was time to go to the Io Valley for their last site seeing outing.

She had picked the restaurants for their last two evening sessions and had finalized the last two breakfast places she wanted to try. She had targeted the many ways that pancakes could be prepared, and each experience had been a pleasant surprise.

She joked with Matt that she was making breakfast memories that would weigh heavy and would be hard to forget because if she was not careful she would be wearing them for a long time.

Lunches and dinners proved to be delightful as she tried all the meal items that had a Hawaiian twist. She wondered how many of the variations were really Hawaiian or just the imagination of very good chef's. She decided that the answer was not important. She just added more jogging to her daily activity to counter all the good food.

Every morning, she would weigh herself on the very expensive digital scale in the lavish master bathroom and was pleased that the running was keeping her from gaining the weight she had feared she would.

Io Valley was a great place for a casual walk. She held Matt by the hand on the flat surfaces but jogged the steps on the way up and down.

She was not expecting anyone to call her, and almost missed the incoming call as she dug through her be belly bag for her phone.

She had at first thought about ignoring it, but something drove her to answer it.

She soon knew that her magnet to attract strange criminal behavior was working and she realized she had no control over that magnet even though she was trying to keep it turned off.

She listened as the person calling introduced herself as, Leilani Dickens, Chief of Maui detectives band requested a meeting. She offered to buy lunch at a location of Alex's choice.

Alex had already selected one of the most expensive restaurants for the next day's lunch. She did not want to change that to some other venue, so she suggested they do breakfast at nine the following morning and gave the address of the breakfast spot that she had selected.

She hung up and looked at Matt who had been standing at the rail looking at the needle like peak that stood between two taller ones and commented that she had left her criminal attraction magnet on.

He smiled and said that she didn't need a magnet to attract him, since he was already as close as he could be to the magnetic woman of his dreams.

Alex gave him hug and said that the man of iron that she loved was welcome to be as close to her magnet as he chose to be. She held his hand and continued their walk through the park.

Io Valley would be the last touristy place, but they had another swim on their private beach and the pleasure of a majestic house.

That evening, after a long run along the road through the lava field, she sat down and sent the Chief and Johnnie a text letting them know that their presentation to the police convention had reached into the middle of the Pacific Ocean and the rip tide they had generated was pulling her in.

She explained that the Maui Chief of Detectives had approached her about helping out with a case involving a string of missing persons and they suspected they had a serial killer on Maui but had run into a wall in trying to solve the case.

She let them know that she was meeting with her in the morning for breakfast.

The next morning, she and Matt arrived early to the restaurant. Alex selected a table that was to one corner of the outdoor patio. She wanted to be as isolated as possible from the rest of the patrons.

She watched three persons arrive a few minutes before nine and stood up and waved to them. For once she would not be the smallest of the people in the group. As they greeted each other and made introductions, she took note that Matt stood out and looked like a father figure standing over a group of children. Even sitting down, he stood out.

Alex ordered Hawaiian passion fruit pancakes with two eggs and sausage on top. She put plenty of butter between each pancake and slathered on guava preserves.

She smiled as Malia commented that she was eating pancakes in the Hawaiian fashion.

Matt commented that other than the type of pancakes, Alex was eating pancakes in Alex's normal fashion.

Leilani said that after breakfast she would share the details of the case and she hoped that Alex could help them figure out how to solve it.

The arrival of the food took their initial attention. After a few bites, Alex asked David how long he had been a detective.

After asking a similar question of the other two, she learned that she had as many years being a detective as the three Maui detectives had in total.

She realized that she had been solving cases at a rapid pace and time had swirled and passed around her like the water swiftly rushing down very steep rapids.

She didn't feel old.

Her first case seemed like it had only happened a few days before.

She looked at Matt and realized that they had been together more than half that time and she still thought of their being together as something that was fresh and new.

Then she smiled and thought about all the memories that together they had already made. She knew that together they were keeping everything fresh and new.

She turned her attention to Leilani as she gave the general outline of the case and David, and Malia added the details.

She knew almost immediately how she would approach helping them.

It seemed so obvious to her and yet she understood how they could have missed the key ingredient that might lead to the solution.

She also knew that getting to the solution would take exceptional sleuthing.

Leilani closed the discussion with the question for which she hoped to get a yes.

Can you help us?

Alex suggested that Leilani should call her Chief and convince him to let her stay to help and yes she had several ideas of how the case would be solved.

Alex gave Leilani a slip of paper that had Chief Bruce Lincoln Johnson written on one side and his phone number on the other side.

She said that the Chief would know how to handle a call from Leilani.

She ended by saying that she was going to let her Chief, talk with the Maui Chief and the two of them could work out the agreement of her involvement.

She went on to say that if she were to get involved she wanted to ensure that her IT was part of the agreement.

David blurted out and asked, "what did Malia and I was miss?"

It was clear to Alex that she would have to give both David and Malia a way to reconcile their failure and not lose face.

Alex smiled and complemented he and Malia on their thoroughness, but she said that her secret weapon was that she had the help of a miracle worker that would help all of them go where none of them had been.

And she added that they would need to go there to solve the case.

Leilani smiled and asked if the miracle worker happened to be the old Vietnamese War Veteran that she had met at the convention, who she had chatted with and who had convinced her to buy the video clip he was so proud of.

Alex nodded and complimented Leilani on her keen observation. She reiterated that if her Chief was convinced and when her miracle worker led them to the solution, Leilani would be looking for an IT miracle worker with Johnnie's talents.

She smiled when Leilani asked what it would take to lure him to Hawaii. She replied that Leilani would have to bake cookies that were superior to hers.

Alex then explained that her vacation ended in two days and she and Matt had added jogging each of Maui's beaches and were in the process of trying to accomplish that goal in their final few hours.

She pointed out that if she were to stay, she would need to know rather soon so she could see about either continuing to stay at the place she was staying or try to find some other similar attractive accommodation.

Leilani replied that she had a place that was right on the beach where Alex could stay and that she would arrange her stay as soon as it was clear that Alex's Chief would accept her request. She gave the address and said that Alex should drive by and take a look to see if the house would meet her standards. She said she didn't think she could match the red Jaguar that she had parked next to in the parking lot but then cars were easy to hold on to.

Alex nodded and replied that possession was two thirds of the law, and she would hold on to her rental car.

They all walked out together to their cars and Alex turned left from the parking lot and Leilani turned right.

Matt smiled and commented that his magnetic woman had handled the situation superbly. He then said that from the look he had seen on her face, he most likely would be flying back to Cincinnati on his own.

He asked her what she thought was the problem with the current investigation.

Alex looked at Matt and said that she was not playing poker with him any longer if he could so easily read her thoughts.

Then she shared that most serial killers didn't ramp up their killing when they start out. Instead, they killed and then they waited to see if they were discovered. The wait could be months or years. She figured that if she had Johnnie go back several years and analyze the missing persons records, he might be able to find some connection with previous missing person's reports and the current uptick in the number of missing persons.

She pointed out that none of the bodies of the missing persons in the case had ever been found and she felt that was also very important.

She parked the car, and they began the day's beach jogging activities.

Alex was still working on her Passion Fruit, Guava flavored Shaved Ice as she and Matt walked back along the Mai Poina Beach when she spotted Leilani, Malia, and David walking toward them. She noted that they had their shoes off and they all had a smiles on their faces.

She was surprised at how fast Leilani had reached a deal with the Chief.

She at first wondered how they had found her and then she remembered that her red Jaguar was parked on the side of the road.

By the look on their faces, Alex knew that she would be staying. She greeted them with, "yes, it will be wonderful to stay and work with a team that casually strolls down beaches and calls it work."

Leilani replied that Alex's Chief was a tough negotiator but agreed to having her stay as long as she, Alex agreed to the deal. He had insisted that all expenses would be covered by the island budget and that the living accommodations had to be equivalent to what Alex had set up for herself.

Leilani smiled and said that the house at the seaside of Keawakapu Beach that had been confiscated from a drug distributor was as luxurious as the one she was currently in but of course it was not as secluded and might not have the same charm.

She hoped that Alex would find it acceptable.

Leilani then asked if she could treat the two of them to some sushi and a drink.

Alex replied that neither of them had eaten lunch and that Sushi sounded great.

During lunch Leilani suggested that Alex move in after seeing Matt off. She would arrange the move and she would get whatever Alex wanted as food and snacks.

Alex said that there was plenty of food that just needed to be moved from one refrigerator to another.

She thanked her for making the arrangements and said that she and Matt would stop by and look over the house. She was sure that the two of them had jogged by it earlier that day but at that time she had no clue that she would be staying in any of the houses along that beach.

After their late lunch, Alex drove to the address and opened the gate with the remote that Leilani had given her. She drove in and parked. The lawn around the house was golf green soft and smooth. She led the way around the house and admired the flowers planted along the edges of the yard. The black iron fence across the yard that faced the beach was at least a foot taller than Matt and had spikes at the top.

They entered the house and surprised a young lady that was cleaning the kitchen. Alex greeted her with an Aloha and said that she would be moving in the next day and was just looking the place over.

She felt the décor was impeccable and gave the place an impressive, rich look but it did not have the charm of the current home that she had rented.

Matt said that it was high end but commented it did not have the charm and was not as warm and inviting as the house where the two of them had spent their vacation.

She suggested they return to their current house and go snorkeling one more time in their private swim area.

The next day was move out day. Alex fixed her favorite breakfast for both of them, and they ate out on the veranda and enjoyed the morning breeze and the sounds of the ocean.

She asked Matt whether she should see if the house was for sale and if it was what he thought about the two of them buying it.

Matt said he would love to have such a place and he had a nice amount saved but there was no way that he could see having enough money to pay for such a place.

Alex told him that she had the leverage to get a very large loan, but she worried about ability to pay the monthly bill as well.

She said that she was going to work on it if he liked the place enough to come back at least once a year.

Matt looked at her and smiled and said that he would love to come with her at least that often and he knew that knowing her, the odds were that he would be doing so, and she would be the owner.

She listened as Matt then recounted all the great memories they had experienced together.

He then told her to be careful on the case she was getting involved in and that the killer had to be crafty to have kept from getting caught.

Alex assured him that she, as always, intended to take all safety precautions. She let him know that she would be working with Johnnie to dig deeper into the missing person's data to see if they could find the original kill that started the current cycle of missing persons.

The drive to the airport was rather silent and Alex kept thinking of all the good times they had enjoyed on Maui. Other than a hat and one shirt or blouse, they were taking no other souvenirs back to Cincinnati.

At the airport, after getting the luggage out of the car, Alex gave Matt a hug and a long kiss and wished him a good flight home. She watched him pull his luggage over to the agricultural inspection station and lift it onto the belt that took his suitcase through a scanner. After waving one more time she watched Matt walk into the ticket area.

She got into the car and drove slowly out of the airport. She realized she was already missing Matt. She thought over all the fun they had enjoyed together and knew that taking vacation together in Hawaii had been a great decision.

She had spent lavishly and was glad of it. She had enjoyed having someone around to talk to and share the beautiful island.

She knew that she had spent the right amount of time to make memories.

While at the airport side of the island she headed to the Police station address that Leilani had provided.

Her unannounced arrival caused a momentary delay as the receptionist checked to see if Leilani was available. A few moments later she was escorted to Leilani's office where she was greeted and offered a cup of coffee.

Leilani said that she was surprised but pleased to see her.

Alex let her know that she would spend the day getting oriented to her new abode and to the details of the case. First, she would move into the house that was being provided. She then would review the current case in detail, and she wondered if Malia and David could be available for lunch and then do the detailed review of the case at the safe house.

Leilani said that working with her on her time as she wanted was what the two would be expected to do. She asked Alex to take the lead and Malia and David would provide the support.

Alex asked for the password and security information necessary to get her analyst into the Maui, Hawaii data base system.

Leilani called her support and asked her to provide the information and an IT contact person as well.

Once Alex had the information she needed, she went out to where David and Malia were sitting at their desks. She invited them to lunch and let them know that afterwards she wanted to get into the case in detail and they would all sit out on the veranda at the safe-house, relax, and enjoy doing their work.

She then extended an invitation to them to stay at the house with her.

David thanked her but declined because he had other plans.

Malia said she would love to stay at the house and would bring a suitcase with the essentials when she came over.

Alex then asked that the two of them to move their white board and all their evidence into the study in the safe-house. She said that she wanted to get started late in the afternoon and review everything they had.

David asked why she wanted to go through what he and Malia had done when it had taken them to a dead end.

Alex replied that she wanted to understand both ends of the hockey stick that made up the case. She again complemented he and Malia on having done a good piece of the work on the case.

She then let them know that before lunch she was going to be at the safe-house house talking with her Chief and getting her miracle worker on board.

She asked Malia to select a restaurant for lunch. She said that she preferred they focus on Mom and Pop restaurants that Malia and David thought were good or ones they wanted to try. If there was some fancy restaurant that either of them had been avoiding due to the cost, she volunteered to buy.

Malia asked if it was OK to go to a relative's restaurant because some of her relatives and some of David's relatives ran small but good places.

Alex said she actually preferred trying them first. She said that often she ate the best meals at such places.

Malia said she would set up meals at all her and David's relative's restaurants before moving on to other favorites.

Alex let the two know that she was off to make sure her car rental could be extended and that her house rental was properly closed. She would then be at the safe-house and then meet them at the restaurant that was selected for lunch.

<u>5 Miracle Worker</u>

Both the car rental and the seaside home rental offices were near the police station, so Alex decided to stop at each before driving back to the Wailea area.

The car rental was a quick and an automatic renewal for another two weeks. The car rental was actually pleased to keep it rented out since the upper end cars often were past up for the larger ones or less expensive ones.

The visit to the realtor that managed the house she had just finished renting took a little longer because Alex inquired whether the home was for sale.

She was surprised that it was on the market but not being advertised at the moment since it was the high season for rentals.

She asked what the price of the home would be when it was to be advertised. She wrote down what the asking price was and let the realtor know that she was interested in the house and would get back to her once she was ready to make an offer.

She went out to her car and decided to call her mother and ask for some home buying advice. She reached her mother at her office and asked her what she thought about her buying a house in Maui.

Her mother was immediately supportive and said that she would love to partner up with her in the purchase. She shared the fact that her father had recently rejected buying a place in Florida, but she was sure he would support a Hawaii purchase.

She went on to say that she would ask one of her firm's associates that specialized in real estate to look into the property and let her know if the asking price was reasonable and what the appropriate offer should be. She said that she would call back the following day and let her know what the offer for the home should be in the current market.

Alex thanked her and said that it would be great to have a partner to buy the home.

She sent an e-mail to Matt to let him know that he had been right about her and that she was getting the support of her parents in her quest for their dream vacation home.

She sat for a moment and let her mind run through what it would take to own what she was thinking was her dream house.

She then drove back to the safe-house and as she drove into the driveway, she thought that perhaps she should ask Leilani whether it was for sale. She was not sure she wanted to make an offer, but she figured it would be useful to have the information about the cost.

It was clear to her that she was going to become a Maui homeowner.

Once at the safe-house she placed a call to the Chief. She listened as he recounted his conversation with Leilani and her plea to allow her to stay and help solve the case that Leilani was sure was a serial killer at work.

He had let Leilani know that it was not up to him but up to his star detective to make the choice and if Leilani had his phone number then the call was about the two of them agreeing to the specifics of who would pay for the participation.

He then shared that he had insisted that Leilani provide a place as comparable to the one that had been rented for vacation. He said that Leilani assured him that she had a plush beach front home that was comparable.

Alex let him know that Leilani had indeed provided a very elegant place and had clarified that she would cover all expenses including the car rental. She said that she could not directly cover the salary, but she would arrange for a grant to the Cincinnati detective budget that would cover most of the salary, but she was not sure she could cover it all and wondered if national recognition of a successful case would be of some value.

Alex listened as the Chief let her know that he had run that up the line and everyone thought it was a very good deal and that it would provide great recognition for Cincinnati.

Alex chuckled and said that now all she had to do was to solve a case that three very capable detectives in Maui had failed to do.

She thanked the Chief for having such high confidence in her ability and said she had to get to her miracle worker and get him to provide her the breakthrough information that would solve the case.

The Chief said that Johnnie's time would also be covered by Leilani so she should make sure that he kept track of the time he time spent on the case.

Alex then called Johnnie and shared the situation with him.

He thanked her for having arranged access to the Hawaiian police data bases and other databases. He said having an IT contact in Hawaii would most likely make it easy to get to all the data.

He then asked what he would be looking for and how he should approach the data analysis.

Alex said that currently the team on the case had only gone back one year from the time the uptick in missing persons had taken place. She described the upward slope of new cases as that of the upward slope of a hockey stick, but they had not gone back far enough to identify the long handle of the hockey stick.

She felt they were missing the point in time when the killer had started to kill.

She figured that it had started as some sort of revenge against some tormentor or tormentors.

She speculated that the first few killings had ignited the feeling of power that led the killer to continue and that the feeling probably began to fade and like a drug addict he needed more of the feeling of power he got from killing his victim.

She likened it to a drug that slowly lost its effect on the body and the person needed to get a larger dose of the medicine.

She figured the upward slope was because the killer needed more stimulation and that he had perfected his killing technique and believed that he would not get caught.

She suggested seeing if any of the missing person reports that went back a few years had individuals that went to the same High School or University. If he found these victims, he should look into their association with each other and how they were viewed by their classmates.

She said that she was looking for a bully and anyone that supported the bully or was associated with the bully, and she thought that one of the people that had been bullied was probably the killer.

Johnnie commented that he had joined the Marines because he had been bullied as a young kid and that he still had thoughts of getting even with the bully. He said he also remembered the one person who, though he was white, had defended him against that bully and had actually shielded him for the rest of his time in high school. He said he knew exactly who he was looking for.

She pointed out that most missing person's reports usually found a body or had an explanation like the person was swept out to sea. In the current case, no bodies had been found and there was almost the same number of men and women victims.

This indicated to her that it was not about sex but about inflicting pain or torture. It also indicated to her that the killer most likely worked in the service sector that allowed him to identify his next victim.

Johnnie said he had the idea and would begin his search at least several years back and work toward the information that had already been detailed and sorted. He said that he would partner with the local IT so that Alex would have up to the moment access to what he learned, and Maui would have a person who knew how to organize data for the detective unit.

Alex thanked him and promised all the cookies he might want when he provided her with the most likely suspect.

Johnnie gave his signature tough guy laugh and said that he would work extra hard and at ultra-speed to make sure he got a tray of cookies.

Alex hung up feeling confident that she would have the information that would allow her to solve the case in a relatively short time.

As she thought about time, she realized that she had seen one missing person's report that mentioned the full moon. The next full moon was only a few days away.

The connection to the moon cycle would be the first thing that she would have the three of them validate.

She wondered if she should drive to the safe-house, and she was trying to decide when a text from Malia provided the lunch address and said that it was a food truck run by her cousin and that he had some wonderful Hawaiian Fish Tacos and a great assortment of juices.

Alex replied that it would only take her about five minutes, and she would be there. When she arrived, Malia waved her over to a picnic table that she was holding.

Alex walked over and joined her as David got to the table with a plate that had at least ten fish tacos on it. He said that what the two of them needed to do was to get the drinks they desired and to bring him a large lemonade.

Once she got back to the table, David asked what he and Malia had missed in investigating their case and what Alex would do that was different.

Alex shared the hockey stick analogy and said that she had her miracle worker looking back along the long handle of the hockey stick for the first few occurrences of missing person reports that would define the beginning of the killings.

The fact that there were so few missing person's reports before the uptick would simplify the search, but the trick would be to identify the potential killer.

She went on to say that she had profiled him to be in his twenties or early thirties, was a lower-level service employee who had started out on the road to being a serial killer by killing some adversary or adversaries that had somehow tormented or bullied him.

Malia stopped her and asked where she had learned to profile a potential killer that she had never met.

Alex explained that it was a well-tested approach used to identify criminals and killers used by many police departments. She said that she had gotten her training from a renowned profiler that was a professor at her university, and later he had given several training sessions to the Cincinnati detective unit members. She asked if Hawaii had access to someone like that. If not, she would give her the name of the professor that was an excellent and talented profiler.

Malia said she was going to follow up to see if they could get similar training.

Alex went on to explain that she had requested Johnnie to see if the missing persons might have gone to the same school. She felt that high school, a high school bully or bullies or those that ran with the bully might be some of the missing persons.

She hoped that Johnnie would quickly identify these persons because she seemed to recall from the cursory review of the case that she had done, the timing of the most recent killings correlated to the full moon and that a full moon was only two or three days away.

David gave a small laugh and asked if she was expecting to solve the case so quickly? He went on to say that if she did then the fact that the previous investigation and the one that he and Malia had been doing had cost the lives of at least ten people.

Alex nodded and said she knew how he felt about that and that there was no way to change the past. She knew the feeling and that she had at first let it take her down, but she had recovered because she had great support and a team that learned to react quickly and with the precision that solved cases and saved lives.

She reiterated that all of them worked at saving lives and the three of them were going to do it together.

The killer was responsible for the deaths.

Their job was to do their job as best they could to prevent the next death.

Alex refilled her sweet tea and took a moment to complement Malia's cousin for his great fish tacos. She paid for the lunch and left a generous tip as well.

She then suggested they all go back to the safe-house, change into their swimsuits, and take a dip in the ocean before getting into the details of the case.

Malia commented that she was beginning to understand why Alex had her Chief supporting whatever she wanted to do.

Alex shook her head and said that it was not about personality. It was about successfully closing cases and making her Chief look good.

Alex pointed out that success allowed him to influence his leaders to support what the department needed to do, and it led to him letting her do what she chose to do.

David looked at her and suggested that she had learned to guide her Chief in such a manner that he always looked good even when there might be some disagreement between them.

Alex nodded and added that Chief's had one hand in politics and the other on the work that needed to get done. She made the point that she just freed up the work hand and gave him two hands to handle the politics.

David looked at Malia and commented that they would have to figure out how to free up Leilani's work hand and let her have two hands for the politics of the department.

Malia nodded and said that lately she had probably made it necessary for Leilani to have two hands handling the work side and she personally needed to take action to change that relationship that had the two of them often facing off against each other.

Alex quietly said that her approach was to treat others as she wished to be treated. It was that simple though it often was hard when emotions ran high.

After the swim they returned to the safe-house, and Alex had the two share the details of their report. She asked that the dates of the missing persons reports, and the moon cycle be coordinated.

She had made some iced tea and they all sat on the Veranda enjoying it and some snacks as a cool sea breeze blew gently up toward the house.

Alex listened as the two of them explained what they had done and how they felt like the blind man who felt a donkey's tail and then described the animal.

She pointed at the sun that was now slowly moving toward Lanai located slightly to the right of the veranda and outlined above the darker blue of the ocean. She then pointed at the faint outline of the almost white moon and then she pointed to the chart that matched the full moon dates to the missing person's report dates. The lines visually showed there was an almost a perfect correlation.

David nodded and said that he and Malia had missed the correlation to the moon and now that they had plotted it seemed to be very important.

Alex nodded and said that the full moon was only a few days away and that was all the time they had to save the next victim.

She then said it was time to quit for the day and asked where they were going to have dinner.

David said that it would be in a small ten table restaurant run by his aunt. She served a family style meal, and the only variation was in the meat that one chose. He said the choice of meats were beef, lamb, goat, and pork and there was a choice of baked or mashed potatoes. Everything was brought to the table and shared family style, and you could have all you could eat for one price but had to clean your plate to get more.

Alex suggested that they all go together, and she would drive the short distance into Kihei, and David would give the directions to the restaurant.

When they walked in, and Alex commented on the family atmosphere feel of the place and then settled in for what she knew would be a great meal.

Once the family greetings were over, they all took a table that was against the far wall.

The meal was as good as David had promised. Alex had chosen goat and enjoyed its savory taste.

She later complemented David's aunt on the great meal, and she left a generous tip.

After they returned to the safe-house, Alex said she was going out for a jog before calling it a day.

David said he would pass on the run and would meet them at breakfast the next morning at eight.

Malia asked whether she could join in on the jog. She said she was not sure she could keep up but wanted to try.

Alex led the way along the walk that led to Ula beach. She kept the pace slow and steady, and she asked Malia about herself and then listened as Malia shared her childhood and her school experience.

When they reached Ula beach, she stopped and walked the wooden walkway and stopped to admire the view.

Malia asked about Alex's family and what it was like growing up on the mainland.

Alex decided to share only a few simple details because she realized that her youthful experiences were those of a rich person and might make her sound condescending.

She took up a slightly faster pace on the way back to minimize the talking.

She jumped into the shower and let the hot spray hit. She could feel the tension, which had been building since she had made the correlation to the cycle of the moon, slowly leave.

She knew this feeling. It always took place when she knew that a life hung in the balance and if she did not act swiftly that life could be lost.

She had just come out of the shower and was getting ready to get to bed when she got a call from Johnnie.

She quickly did the math and realized that it was three in the morning in Cincinnati and that Johnnie had yet to go to sleep.

She told him to go and get some rest.

Johnnie said that he would do so as soon as they were done talking but he wanted to share the names of the first missing persons that fit into the "no body found category." He then gave her their names.

He also wanted to give her the names of the three persons who had gone to the same school, as that of the two missing persons, who might fit the bill as the killer. He then gave her the names and addresses of the three.

Finally, he added the name of the high school that was common to all three. He told her he was packaging up everything he had and sending it to her via e-mail.

Alex thanked him and promised that he had two cookie trays on credit in his account but he needed to get to bed and get some sleep so he would be alive to eat them.

He laughed and replied that he was off to sleep and would not wake up until noon.

After she hung up Alex went to the kitchen and set up the coffee maker so that she would have hot coffee ready when she got up.

She resisted getting on her computer to retrieve her e-mail because she knew she would not be able to stop once she got into the information that Johnnie had sent.

She knew that, at breakfast the next day, she was going to surprise the doubting David with the information that Johnnie had provided.

She felt that she was within a day or two of "getting her man." And she knew that the killer indeed was a man and she desperately wanted to save the next victim and at the same time catch him in the act of trying to kill that victim.

She wanted him dead to rights.

It took her a long time to fall asleep.

She went into mentally planning what to do.

She planned the review of the information that Johnnie had sent.

She planned a trip to the high school to look at the appropriate year books to see if the first victims could be identified.

She then wanted to get a firsthand look at the three potential suspects themselves.

She did not remember falling asleep, but she awoke looking forward to the day's events.

Little did she realize how important the day would prove to be.

5 Miracle Worker

6 The Killer

*O*kina spent the evening enjoying the videos of his first two swims at the waterfall pool. He always made it a popcorn and beer event accompanied by some snappy upbeat music.

He had tried a variety of ways to enjoy the videos and had decided that he liked his current approach best. It always put him in a better mood.

He periodically played some of the more recent swimming events, but they did not hold the same bang that the first two did. This habit had satisfied him for almost a year.

He had realized he needed more swimming and to swim more often. He then began to swim once a month when the moon was full. He could have picked any day to swim but the full moon provided the amount of light that resulted in good pictures.

He now spent the month selecting the next person to go into the basket.

He was now confident that he had devised the perfect way of continuing enjoying his monthly swim in a pool of blood. He was very careful and discrete, so he was confident that his activities were going unnoticed.

He was ready for the next full moon.

He had found the next swim partner when he was in line waiting to check out his groceries. The person ahead of him kept berating the checkout clerk for going too slow or mischarging her for what was being scanned, her attitude and her derogatory words put her on his swim list. She seemed to think she was superior.

She acted like a bully.

He backed out of the checkout lane and put his cart at the end of the isle. Then he went out of the grocery store and waited for her to go to her car. He got her car license plate number and followed her as she left.

He was correct in assuming that she would go home to put away her groceries.

He now had an address as well.

He would spent the rest of the month watching what she did at home and where she went to work during the day.

He had come to realize that the tracking and the preparation period was almost as enjoyable as the swim.

Finding and then determining how to get the victim into the basket was a challenge that grabbed hold of him and seemed to give him the purpose that he otherwise lacked.

So far each of the persons that had stood in the basket had provided him the scenario that allowed him to get them there almost risk free. He looked in her mailbox and knew that her name was Yvonne and by watching from his car, he learned that she drank wine almost every night and then fell asleep with the television on.

He looked up at the almost full moon and felt good about being ready. The swim would reinvigorate and renew the feeling of having achieved his goals in life.

The feeling of power seemed to flow into him as he enjoyed the video of his first swim. He ate a handful of popcorn and followed it with a gulp of beer. He was going to enjoy another relaxing evening.

Alex's phone sounded her mother's signature drumbeat. Her mother was calling about the purchase of the house that she was interested in.

Her mother told her that the junior partner at the firm that specialized in the housing market had determined that the offer for the house they were interested in should be at least one hundred thousand less than the amount the realtor had shared.

She then said that if getting the money in hand quickly was of interest to the seller, they could deliver a certified cashier's check for the offered amount on the same day as they made the offer. Delivering the check would be contingent on getting the deed being turned over to the bank.

After more or less blurting out that it had been a fast turnaround, Alex said that she really appreciated it. She asked what her dad thought about the purchase.

Her mother replied that her father was all for the purchase and said he was looking forward to coming out to make sure it was as wonderful as Alex had made it sound.

Alex laughed and said that she would call the realtor and make the offer and they would all soon know if they would be landowners in Hawaii.

She mentioned that she was staying at a safe-house that was also on the market, and it was very nice, spacious and had a great view, was in the same price range, but it did not have the charm that the other house had, so she hoped that the offer for it would be accepted.

After again thanking her mother she hung up.

She then sent a text to Matt to say that she was making an offer on their house. She added that he only needed to put up his million dollar share, and they would be home free. She then added JJ after that line.

She later sent another text to explain what JJ meant (Just Joking) so there would be no confusion.

She then made a call to the realtor and said that she was ready to make an offer. She made the offer and let the realtor know that a cashier's check could immediately be written for the amount of the offer contingent on getting the deed into the bank's hand.

The realtor said she would communicate with the current owner and get back to her.

Alex hung up and sipped her coffee and looked at the time. The realtor had been non-committal and she wondered if that meant that the lower offer was not acceptable. Well, she thought it was what it was and there was nothing she could do but wait.

She sent another text to Matt and said that the offer was in and that her parents were going to be part of the purchase and that she had the funds for their share.

It was time to go to breakfast. She felt the day would be a fruitful one.

She called to Malia that it was time to go to breakfast and that she needed directions on how to get there.

At breakfast she went for biscuits and gravy with sausage and two over easy eggs. She had green tea and a small, sweet roll.

She kept teasing David that she was sure that this was the day that they would break the case open.

He was in a good mood, and teased back and challenged her to make a bet that would be worth his time that he could collect the next day.

She countered that she would treat him to a dinner at the most expensive restaurant on Oahu if she lost and pay for the travel there as well as the dinner.

Malia said that she wanted in on the bet, but she wanted to bet on Alex's side.

Alex laughed and said that it was time to get to work.

From the veranda of the safe-house, Alex pointed at the faint white outline of an almost full moon and commented that they needed to take action to prevent the next person from being killed. She said that she was certain that the next victim was just a few days away from his or her death.

She then said they would start with a review of the information that Johnnie had sent and that the information would be what guided their work that day.

She, Malia, and David spent the morning reviewing the information that Johnnie had provided.

David asked how Johnnie had been able to find the connection between the victims, potential perpetrators, and the school.

Alex replied that she called him her miracle worker because once he understood what she was looking for he would devise a variety of ways to parse the data. She said that sometimes she wondered exactly how he was able to get to the information that he found.

She then said that it was time to check on the school connection.

They all rode together in the Jag to the high school where several of the early missing persons had been students. Malia sat in back because David did not fit the back seat very well and it was a perfect fit for her.

Alex commented that she made a great backseat driver.

They arrived at the school and after a brief discussion with the principle to explain that they needed to look at several yearbooks of past classes to see if they could connect some missing persons with the school they had attended.

They were escorted to the library and were able to go through the yearbooks that coincided with the high school years of the people on their list.

Malia found one football player that was on the missing persons list. She commented that he seemed to come across as a bully.

A yearbook or two later showed a picture of a cheer leader who was on the list.

Alex looked back to the picture of the football player and saw the cheer leader in the crowd around him.

She was sure that the date of when the two went missing marked the beginning of the serial killers actions.

She pointed out that the first killing had occurred almost three years ago. Then the second one a little less than two years ago. Then after almost a year things began to shorten up with a killing six months later, then three months and finally it went to the timing of the moon cycle.

David asked how she could be so sure about when it had started.

Alex replied that she was not sure. She said that their next step was to look into the three persons Johnnie had named as potential killers.

She returned to the yearbook and found the picture of one of the potential killers that was a contemporary of the football player. This person had the standard one by two picture that all class members had but he did not show up in any other pictures.

David asked about the other two persons that Johnnie had identified.

They looked through the year books and found one very active in the school theater and the band. The other was a year ahead and had been a football player and had been on the student council.

Alex replied that both of these two potential killers had both gone on to higher education.

One was now a phycologist who was married, had three kids, and was practicing his profession in Seattle. Alex said that the information seemed to exclude him as the killer.

The other was a Manufacturing Plant Manager in California who was also married and had twin daughters and a wife who was a lawyer.

Alex again said that she doubted that either of the two flew to Hawaii on a monthly basis to kill someone.

She said that they would have to look more closely at the third person to see if they could find out more about him.

She was flipping through the yearbook when almost by accident, she found his name in the credits as one of the people that had helped to organize and edit the yearbook.

This caused her to take a closer look at all group photos in all the yearbooks that they had looked through. She found a picture of that person behind the counter in the football concession stand in the yearbook of the previous year of the football star's graduation date.

Alex then verbally did a quick profile of the person who was quietly active in the school environment but remained in the background. He remained mostly in the background but was involved enough that he could easily become the focus of a bully that disliked him. She pointed out that he looked frail and weak. Being bullied would make him resentful and have the desire to get even.

Malia commented that she did not ever want to be hunted by Alex.

Alex said that the three of them were now going on to the next phase of the hunt to verify that the third person was the killer. She said that she felt that he was likely the person who was committing the killings.

She put in a quick call to Johnnie and asked him to find the work address for the number one suspect as soon as possible.

She looked at Malia and asked where they were going to have lunch.

Malia had been expecting the question and said that they were less than five minutes away from her aunt's restaurant that offered a great variety of food.

Once they were at the table, Alex quickly zeroed in on the ox tail soup that she ordered with onion rings, corn bread and tossed greens on the side. She added a Lilikoi as the drink.

After all the orders were in, she said that they would go to wherever their number one suspect worked and observe him in some manner. They would make the call when they learned where he worked.

David complemented Malia on having picked a great place for lunch. He had never been in the place before, but he liked the variety that was on the menu.

He then asked Alex how she was able to get Johnnie to be available on demand.

Alex smiled and replied that she bribed him.

That caused David to pause and then simply say, "really!"

Malia laughed and said that she could verify that Alex indeed did bribe Johnnie and that she had overheard Alex bribing him. She said if questioned in court she would spill the fact that Alex use the ultimate of bribes.

David shook his head and said, "alright give me the punch line."

Malia laughed and said that Alex bribed her IT with trays of cookies.

After a moment, she asked how Alex had developed such a loyal and capable supporter.

Alex smiled and said that it was all very personal in the detective department. They were family and they did not engage in mountains of paperwork and request forms. They just did it. They got it done legally one way or another and they focused on speed.

Time on most of her cases was usually ticking down and at the end when the timer went off and if they did not solve the case, someone died.

She said that each of her team members had saved the other at some time on some case and they all knew it was important to have each other's back. Their work together had created a bond that she knew would hold for a lifetime.

David said that it sounded like a place he would enjoy working.

Alex looked at him and said he was working in a place that she would enjoy working and that he could make the place he was working the place he wanted to be.

She slowly consumed her ox tail soup with bites of a generously buttered corn bread. She put the heap of onion rings in the middle so they could all share them. The Lilikoi passion fruit drink served ice cold, in a frosted glass, was gorgeously delicious.

When Malia's Aunt came around to see how they were enjoying their meal, Alex complemented her and let her know that it was a place she would return to every time she was on the island.

When they got to the car, Malia said that her Aunt had stopped her and asked if the beautiful black lady was some sort of movie star.

Alex laughed and said that it was not going to help Malia one bit to try and butter her up, because of the great meal, the two of them were going to run even faster and farther that evening than they had the previous evening.

The phone rang and Alex stepped back into the shade. She put Johnnie on speaker phone so they could all listen to what he had learned.

He said that the person of primary interest currently worked in a pharmacy during the day and worked at the bar at a hotel near the Black Rock Beach. He went on to say that an expanded search of the data base let him find the several bars where the suspect had previously worked. One of the bars was located at the edge of a middle-class neighborhood and was within a few blocks of the first person listed as missing and the time he worked there was about the same time that the first victim went missing.

Alex thanked him and asked him to send the information he had to her by e-mail.

She hung up and looked at David and asked if he were up for an evening drink at the bar near the Black Rock Beach.

David nodded his agreement and said that it was hard for him to accept that she was making it look so easy to get to the source of the killings.

It made him feel very inadequate as a detective.

Alex looked at him and said that he needed to accept the fact that the case had been handed to him in a fashion that had he and Malia off on the yellow brick road looking the wrong way and that Kansas had been in the other direction and needed a balloon ride to get to.

She had benefited from that and had asked herself what needed to be different. Otherwise, she too might have traveled the same road he had.

David nodded and said that he accepted the fact that she was trying to console him, but it still made him mad at himself.

Malia added she felt the same way but they both should listen to Alex and look forward and focus on saving the next victim.

The address of the pharmacy was only a few blocks away. Alex asked if either of them had a standing prescription at that pharmacy.

The pharmacy was located inside of a large grocery store chain.

Malia said that she had a standing prescription at a branch of the same pharmacy, and she could go in and see what role their potential killer had in the pharmacy.

Alex asked David to stay outside so that he would not be accidentally seen by their suspect and that she would browse the medicine aisles while Malia got a close look at the suspect.

She took her phone out and stood in the aisle as if she were talking and taking a picture of an antiacid bottle. She was able to get a couple of shots of their suspect when Malia walked up to the counter.

Once back outside they all got into the car and Alex drove back to the safe-house.

She asked the two what it would take to organized some back up for them if they needed to move fast.

She wanted to have at least two additional police personnel ready to back them up, and an EMT unit ready to move at a moment's notice. She also wanted to have the suspect under observation twenty four seven for the next several days.

She looked at them and said, "go." It is time to act.

David looked at Malia and smiled and said that this is what they had been waiting for.

They should call their Chief and see if she could deliver as well as Alex's Chief.

Alex smiled and walked to the kitchen where the expresso machine was waiting for her. She had mastered several of its many capabilities. She took her expresso and walked out to the veranda and sat down.

She wondered if Malia's plain tan car was the one that they should use to follow their suspect when he made his move. She thought about it and decided that she would check to see if it was a reliable car.

Her red convertible Jaguar was too flashy and would especially stand out with a full moon in the sky. She figured it would be as bad as having a police car with its lights flashing.

David and Malia came out to the patio and shared the fact that Leilani had been shocked that things were moving so fast and had asked several times if they were sure about the action happening so quickly.

David said that it felt so good insisting that things needed to happen now.

Malia added that Leilani had promised to have people assigned to keep an eye on him twenty four seven and that an EMT unit would be available on call at any time.

Alex then asked about the reliability of Malia's car.

Malia replied that it might looked old, but a mechanic cousin kept it in tip top shape, and it ran like a charm.

Alex asked if she were willing to have it be the car they used to follow the suspect when he made his move.

Malia gave a small laugh and said she would love it if they used her car but after it was over she wanted to have Alex's black handprint put on her trunk with the words she had used in the clip that Leilani had shown them.

Alex gave a small laugh and said she had a deal.

Okani obligingly served the drink to the obnoxious loudmouth at the bar. He wondered if he was a local and asked a few leading questions and learned that indeed he was.

The drunk, as he thought about the loudmouth sitting on the stool, seemed to want to spill his life's story. He babbled about the terrible but well-paying office job where he spent renting cars to obnoxious tourists. He rambled about driving his pickup through rough terrain all way up the mountain. He talked about all the women he had slept with. He finally fell off his stool and passed out on the ground.

Okani came out from behind the bar and took the guy out to his pickup truck that he found by using the keys that he had retrieved from the guys pocket. He got the guys home address off the driver's license and drove to a rather upscale home.

He rang the doorbell to make sure that there was no one else about and then carried the guy who was still passed out into the house.

It was early but he figured this guy was one in whose blood he would swim in next.

He went through the house and located an extra set of keys. He looked through a couple of drawers and found one that had several bar coupons. He looked at the glasses in the cupboard and found several beer glasses from some local bars. He now had an idea of the places this guy drank. It was obvious that he got around. He most probably did not have a steady girlfriend but did have many one nighters.

The house was well appointed, so he knew that the guy made a good salary. He saw a uniform shirt thrown on a chair that gave the name of the car rental where he worked. It was one of the exclusive rental companies that catered to the wealthier clientele.

This bit of information sealed his estimation that the guy was a spoiled ass.

He got the guy up and put him on top of his bed. It was good to know that as he was about to go on his next swim, and that he had the blood supply source for his next moonlight swim identified that would happen the following month.

He went home and enjoyed another evening. He had decided to watch the second video that highlighted Lilanni because it would prepare him for the next woman Yvonne.

7 Moon Light High

Okina got up to go to work and looked out his window at the pale ghost like moon that was very close to being full. The weather service said the full moon would be out the next night.

He had arranged to have the night off at the bar.

He stopped at his victims house. He like her name, Yvonne. He had mentally repeated it often during the month. "Yvonne, Yvonne, Yvonne. It seemed to have a magical ring to him.

Yvonne had her college degree hanging on her living room wall. She also had a picture of her with a megaphone at a football game and seemed to be leading the cheering. This he thought was a step up in caliber of victims for him. He wondered what she was doing working in Maui as a secretary.

He had stopped at her house to up the dose in Yvonne's current bottle of wine. He had lightly dosed all of her bottles; he chuckled to think that he had reduced her alcohol intake because she usually fell asleep after one or two glasses.

He wondered if he dared to propose this to Alcoholics Anonymous.

He gave a little bit of a wild laugh at the thought. He had a way to reduce their alcoholic intake.

For the ones he helped he also knew how to end their drinking problems. "Permanently," he thought and gave another of his cackles.

It was hard for him to concentrate at work. He kept having problems working the register or misunderstanding what medicine the customer was trying to pick up. It made for a long tiring day. By quitting time, he was ready for a drink.

He would have loved a long one but he resisted the urge because he wanted to be sharp so he could enjoy his swim.

He was going to enjoy college level blood. He wondered if it was any better than all the rest that he had enjoyed. He smiled as he thought about swimming in college educated blood.

He would save his drinking and have a great snack maybe a celebratory early morning breakfast after his swim. Maybe he would order a large really rare bloody filet with blood running out into the plate and mix it with buttered mashed potatoes.

He enjoyed the thought, but he decided he would let the evening event guide him on the after swim celebration.

He was hoping for a stellar experience that would satisfy his desire for the next swim for at least the next month.

It was getting harder for him to wait for the full moon. He wondered if there was some alternative to his current approach. He had thought about just anchoring the person in the pool on a long dog chain with their heads just at the water level which would allow the victim to lean their heads back to breath. That would expose their neck and when he sliced their arteries he would create two gushers of blood spurting above the water.

The vision of two gushing and spurting arteries excited him and had him wondering if he should try it with his next victim.

He was enjoying his first video. He looked along the many knives in his display case. He had made it a point to make each knife smaller than the previous one. He was now down to the knife that was only an inch long. He figured he would use a box cutter next and them maybe begin over again with a large, long knife.

He wondered if he should make a second inset display case below the current one. Maybe he should see if another waterfall and pool could become the swim spot for the next series of swim experiences.

He would have to think about how he would continue to enhance his experiences now that he had perfected his swimming stroke.

Alex had put all the safety gear into the trunk of Malia's car. She had insisted that each of them wear a Kevlar jacket and a full bullet proof helmet.

David asked if she expected a gun fight.

Alex made the point that they had no clue what they would face and if there was a gun fight she wanted all of them to be safe.

She shared the fact that in her last case she had her team in two layers of full Kevlar suits from head to toe and only their trigger fingers were left uncovered. Her team had objected to the over kill in protective gear when she had additionally had them wear the police issued body armor and head protection. After a roaring gun battle with a group using AR-15s and each of her them receiving numerous hits and her partner getting hit so many times that his department issued body armor fell off his body, they all had survived and had only suffered some serious bruises. All of her team now vowed to always use the Kevlar body suits if they anticipated a major gun battle.

Malia asked how many time Alex had been hit.

Alex chuckled and commented that on the last case she had been hit multiple times in multiple gun battles. She went on to add that during the gun battle she had just described, as she was laying down to free the victim, she had been hit so many times on a critical part of her body that she was unable to sit down for a week.

David commented that the Kevlar jacket was more comfortable than the standard vest issued by the department. He wondered if the one he had on was going to be his.

Alex replied that the jackets were theirs to use at their discretion, but they should get Leilani to agree to their use.

Malia pointed out that Alex was not having them get into full Kevlar body suits so she must not be putting a major gun battle at the top of the list.

Alex nodded. She commented that this serial killer had been operating for several years with no reports of anyone hearing gunshots. She figured he was killing in some other fashion. Maybe he was smothering, using a knife, or chocking them.

Malia then asked what they were going to do while they waited.

Alex replied that during the day, they would sit on the veranda, take short swims, go to breakfast, lunch, and dinner at the selected restaurants. She finished with saying, "think of the time as a short vacation."

David commented that it sounded great and that he wanted to be on her team.

Alex looked at him and said, "you are on my team."

Malia smiled and said that she was glad to be on the team, but she was going to have to get into better shape to continue to jog with her.

Alex said that in the next few evenings they would drive halfway across the island and park and wait to see which side of the island they would need to get to.

The day was relaxing and the meals, spanned the gamut of countries, covered every imaginable taste and the drinks were of every fruit flavor Alex desired.

She complemented Malia and David for having taken her to such great restaurants.

Late in the afternoon, Malia drove to the midpoint of the island and parked the car on a side road.

Alex got out and took off her long pants, put on her running shoes and asked who wanted to go jogging with her.

She set an easy pace and went out about a mile and returned to where the car was parked. She said she would make a few more rounds. After the second round, David said he would sit the next round out.

Alex upped the pace for the next round and Malia was panting as they got back to the car.

Alex complemented Malia on keeping up and suggested they walk for a few moments before getting back into the car.

There was a gas station on the corner, so they walked there. They bought some gator aid, but their real purpose was to use the restroom.

They were walking back to the car when Alex received a call letting her know that Okina was home and had gone to bed. She thanked the caller and asked him to call her if things changed.

Alex declared the night over and suggested they all go back to the safe-house. She invited David to stay and this time he agreed.

He commented that the run made him realize how out of shape he was and that he really needed to get a good night of sleep so that he could keep up the next night.

The next morning, Alex had just poured herself a cup of coffee when she got a call from the realtor letting her know that her offer had been accepted. She suggested a date when they could meet with the owner, the bank handling the financials and wondered if Alex would have her cashier's check available.

Alex assured her that she would. She sent a text to her mother letting her know that their offer had been accepted.

She sent another text to Matt letting him know that they had the house.

She had just sent her text when she received a call that Okani had stopped at the house of a Yonne Dunn, had gone in and shortly after had left and gone to work at the pharmacy.

Alex asked David to locate the house on the map. It was on the other side of the island from where they were.

She said that their routine that day would be different than the night before.

She commented that Yvonne Dunn was most likely the next victim.

They would have dinner, then go for a jog and afterwards they would go to the other side of the island and would park two blocks away from Yvonne's house.

She would go to the house and make sure that the action was not occurring in the house, and she would run back to the car if Okina was taking Yvonne out of the house.

David asked why they were not arresting Okina before he did anything to Yvonne.

Alex nodded and replied that if they arrested him before they had evidence that he was a serial killer, he might spend the evening in jail, but he would be out the next day and would most likely stop. Then his case would stay on the books until it went cold. During that time Okani would most likely move on and set himself up in some other location.

David nodded and said that he got it.

She looked at Malia and told her to drive slowly when she was following and stay as far back as possible when they drove.

She asked the two of them to get the two additional back up officers that she had requested ready to follow them.

She asked that the support and the EMT units stay five miles behind Malia's car.

She called Leilani and told her that it seemed that the killer was going to make his move that evening and that she would call her once it was confirmed.

She turned Leilani down when asked if she could join in.

She pointed out that Leilani had done a great job getting all the support in place and that her detective team had trained for this moment, and they were ready.

Malia had chosen a top end restaurant saying that if it was the last meal she wanted it to be an expensive one.

Alex agreed and suggested they eat hardy and add an extra mile to the jogging.

David let out a moan and said that he really wanted to try the Steak Bernardin and that following her on a jog afterward would really be difficult.

Alex joked that she would go slow because she was going to order the Kobe beef and of course she would have to have the to die for chocolate-on-chocolate desert cake and a coffee latte.

In fact, she said she would waddle so that they could all keep up.

Malia laughed and commented that Alex's waddle would most likely be equal to her own top running speed.

Alex felt good about how David and Malia were adjusting to her way of leading. She felt comfortable having them as support.

During dinner Alex got a call from the agents tailing Okina saying that he had not gone to work at his bar but had gone home. He was being watched and Alex would get a call when he left the house.

After dinner Alex suggested they go across the Island and chose a place to jog that was close to the house of the potential victim. She said that she wanted to be watching when Okina went into the house in case she needed to take action. She commented that on the fact that Okina had access to the home but had not previously made any effort to go there at night and there had been no cases where neighbors commented about someone making noise, she did not think the action would be in the house.

Once they got to the neighborhood where the house was located they drove past the road and went up the mountain side on what seemed to be a one lane road. She asked Malia to drive to the end to make sure there was no way out. The road ended at a lone house.

She complimented Malia on her three point turn and suggested they park about a half block from the road Yvonne's house was on.

She noted that the road they were parked on was a mix of rocks and gravel of differing sizes and decided against jogging and chose to walk instead.

David thanked her for walking and said that it was hard enough for him to negotiate the stones they were walking across.

Malia commented that she lived in the housing development that was next door to this neighborhood that they were in, and she was amazed at the difference in living standards. There were no sidewalks in her development, but the streets were all wide and of cement.

Alex half listened as she opened the trunk and made sure the Glock 19 was ready and that it was fully loaded. She had only gone to the target range once but had qualified the gun by hitting the bullseye with every shot. If she used it she only planned to shoot once. She hoped to stop the killer and capture him alive.

Malia commented that she was still using her Smith & Wesson 5906 that had been issued to her when she joined the police force.

She commented that there was talk that the Glock models would soon be replacing the Smith & Wesson because replacement parts were getting hard to obtain.

She asked what Alex thought about the Glock.

Alex replied that it was a lighter gun than the 5906 but either gun, when used properly, was acceptable.

She then asked both Malia and David to check their weapons and put on the Kevlar vests. She put on her vest and then her underarm holster and snaped the strap over the Glock's handle.

She was surprised by her phone buzzing in her pocket. It was one of the policemen watching Okina letting her know that Okina was on the move.

Alex reminded the caller that the two of them were to hold well back and let Malia call them in when the action started.

Alex asked that Malia and David get in the car and stay out of sight. She let them know that she was going to get into position somewhere around Yvonne's house.

She made her way slowly up the street hoping that she would not be seen. Once she was at the house she saw that the living room light was on, and the big screen was showing an old movie. She could not see Yvonne.

There were some bushes at the corner just past the back door of the house. She took a position behind them where she was sure she was out of sight but could see the driveway.

As Okina left his house he had to pause a moment after he got into his car.

He was feeling lightheaded.

He had waited what seemed like an eternity for the full moon.

He realized that his need to swim in someone's blood was getting stronger by the day. As he sat and got his bearings back he decided that he was going to move to a two week swim cycle.

He needed it. He knew he was getting worse. He likened it to one's body getting used to a drug and needing stronger and stronger doses.

He drove slowly and made sure that he was making full stops at stop signs. He always was super cautious on his swim nights. He did not want to have any interactions with the law.

He laughed to himself and thought about the fact that he had become a law abiding citizen to make sure he did not get into any police data bases.

He was a more careful driver, never ran traffic lights always parked in designated parking spots, put money in parking meters.

He could share the secret with the police so that they could have safer streets.

He laughed again and drove on.

He always waited until it was as dark as it would get but he tried to make it before it got really late so that his car would not catch the attention of anyone.

He felt that his cautious approach had been one reason that he had never been discovered.

He also knew that his ability to disappear the bodies was another reason that he had not been caught. He had almost filled the initial crevasse that he had been using and wondered whether he should find another one or just start back at the beginning and put another layer of bodies over the previous ones.

He decided that he would figure that out what he would do after the upcoming evening's swim.

He reached the road leading up to Yvonne's house and slowly entered the drive and turned off the headlights. He waited a moment to make sure that no lights went on in any of the surrounding houses.

Once he was sure that no one was watching, he got out and went to the side door and entered the house.

He was confident that Yvonne would be passed out on the couch.

He turned off the television and went to where Yvonne was laying on the couch. She had fallen asleep with wine in her glass that was now a stain on the couch.

He shook his head but decided that it really did not matter. Yvonne would never need to sit on the couch again.

He put the wire tie on her wrists to ensure that he had control and he taped her mouth shut. He made sure she was breathing through her nose then he stood her up and guide her wobbly body out of the living room. He turned off the light in living room as they left.

He guided her to the door and then went out first and pulled her into his arms and then guided her to the car and put her into the passenger's side. Once he had the safety belt on her he went back and closed the side door of the house. He hoped that it would be weeks before anyone decided to come and check on her.

He drove slowly out, again watching the other houses for any lights. There were none and he drove on toward Main Street and then got on highway thirty six and headed toward Hanna.

He was one of a few cars on the road and figured there would be even fewer cars when he left the airport area.

When he got to the point where highway thirty six turned to highway three sixty he knew he was close to getting to swim in a pool of Yvonne's blood.

He drove to the spot where he always parked his car and then moved some of the palm leaves so that his car was out of sight from the road.

He watched an old lady drive by in an equally old car.

He carried his camara tri-pod and basket and went up and put them in place. He then took Yvonne out of the car. She was coming around and began to struggle. He gave her a solid slap across the face and wagged his finger to indicates she should stop. He bent down and quickly snapped on the ankle cuff with the attached chain to her left ankle.

He then looked around to make sure that there were no other people at the falls and took her zip locked hands and guide her up the trail.

He had determined that taking anyone up the face of the falls to the top of the fall would be almost impossible. That was the climb he always made when his victim was in the basket and providing the pool with blood. He would make that climb at least a half a dozen times as he relished every jump from the rocks above.

He got to the top and positioned Yvonne on the top of one of the rocks and stepped down into the basket.

He then pulled Yvonne down into the basked and snaped the ankle chain to the wire mesh. She was once again struggling, and he again gave her a resounding slap. He took the small, bladed knife out and carefully cut her dress off and threw it up on the rocks. He admired her body and saw that she had several tattoos that decorated several sexual body parts. He complemented her on her tattoos and let her know that the maggots would enjoy them.

He really wished he could risk taking the tape off of her mouth so he could hear her beg and scream.

He took off his t-shirt and threw it on the rocks.

He thought back to all the cutting knives he had used. He had started with a huge bowie knife and had slowly worked down to the tiny but razor sharp knife he now held in his hand.

He had cut himself with the straight razor that he had used on one of his swimming partners and had decided to stick with knives.

He was now ready to begin snicking and making small slices along Yvonne's body.

Alex had Malia slow down after passing the point where Okina had pulled off. She jumped out and ran back to where Okina was just taking some equipment up a path that began at the end of the parking area. The moonlight was bright enough for her to see but she was not sure that her phone camera would take a good enough picture in the video mode. She had turned off the automatic light and set the phone so would not put on its light.

She followed him up as he carried his basket and tripod. She watched Okani preparing the basket in the flow of water and hooking it to a chain that he had anchored to an upstream rock and setting up the tripod and checking the picture in his camera.

She then watched from behind a boulder, as he pulled Yvonne into the basket and chained her ankle to it. Now, both of them were standing in the basket with water up to their knees. He was describing what he was going to do and as he ripped and cut Yvonne's dress off.

Alex kept filming as Okani described what he was going to do to Yvonne. When she jumped onto the rock above him and told him to freeze and that he was under arrest he screamed out a long, loud, continuous, "Noooo...."

He looked like he was a wolf howling to the moon. He was going for Yvonne's throat with the knife in his hand when She pulled the trigger. She watched as the knife fell from his hand. She was immediately in the basket between he and Yvonne.

The impact of the bullet seemed to have caused him to stagger back from where he was standing and tumble down into the pool below.

David and Malia were standing behind Alex He said that he would check to see if Okani was still alive.

Alex told him not to worry about Okani because he was swimming in a pool of blood as he had wished only this time it was his own blood. She told David that Okani was dead, and they should focus on getting Yvonne freed and clothed.

She gave Yvonne a hug and told her she was safe. She asked Malia to bring up the blanket that was in the trunk of her car and to tell their backup to fish Okani out and get the keys to the lock holding Yvonne in the basket.

The EMT vehicle arrived and turned on its lights and came up with some emergency clothes that they gave to Alex who was in her protective mode as she then helped Yvonne get dressed.

She suggested that Malia ride with Yvonne to the hospital and stay with her until she was released. They could all meet at Yvonne's house and get her side of the story for their report.

She said that afterward they would all go out for breakfast. Then they would finish their reports and spend the rest of the day sleeping.

She looked at David and said, "Solved in four days. You owe me dinner." and led the way back down the path to the pool below.

8 Final Swim

lex led the way down the path to the pool below. She approached the two police backups and thanked them for their support.

The older officer said that other than fishing a dead guy out of the pool and going through his swimsuit pockets to get the key that had been requested they had done little to help.

Alex stopped him and shared the fact that she felt well supported by the two. They had given her a heads up when the dead man had left his house. They had spent hours following him, and then to be willing to stay back as requested fit the bill as excellent support.

He thanked her and asked who had shot him and that he needed to have that weapon.

Alex gave him the Glock 19 and separately she handed him the cartridge case that she had removed. She then threw in the spent shell of the one bullet she had fired.

The younger officer asked her if it was true, she could hit a target's bullseye with her eyes shut.

She gave a little laugh and said that yes, she had done it once, but she preferred to shoot with her eyes open.

The older officer asked why she had shot the dead guy in the eye.

Alex replied that she had to shoot past the potential victim's head and the eye was the only shot she felt was safe and would immediately kill him before he could wield his knife to kill the victim.

He commented that the Glock had blown out the lower part of the killer's head. They had divers coming out to gather the skull fragments and to recover the knife. He said he was going to be interested in the coroner's report.

He asked what she thought of the Glock.

Alex responded that it was not the gun that was important but the skill of the person using it. She said that during a normal week she spent a minimum of two hours at the range but spaced out, so she was there about every other day. She added that her partner was at her side every time.

The older officer wondered if the range manager ever commented on how often she came.

She gave a little laugh and said that she bribed the range manager with cookies and rolls and was always well received.

David had been listening and commented that in a very short time he had learned more from her than he had for all the years he had been on the force.

Alex thanked him for the complement and challenged him to learn from his partner and from his boss and to learn something from every person he met. She added that if he learned just a small bit from each person, she knew soon he would be seen as having great wisdom. It was all there for an individual to harvest and grow.

David led the way back to the car and the two drove to the hospital where Yvonne had been taken.

Malia greeted them and led them to the room that Yvonne was in.

Alex asked her how she was doing.

Yvonne asked why she had been picked.

Alex said that she was not yet sure but somehow, she fit the profile that triggered the killer. Alex asked if Yvonne had recently berated anyone or made fun of someone.

Yvonne thought for a moment and said that about a month ago she had been rushing to get her grocery shopping done over her lunch break and had lost her temper with the checkout clerk that kept making mistakes during the checkout process. But she pointed out that he was not the person who had taken her to the waterfall.

Alex nodded and said that her berating of the checkout clerk was probably observed by the killer, and she became his target.

Alex pointed out that the killer had a key to her house and asked if she had ever seen him before or if he had ever been to her house.

Yvonne replied that she had no idea how he had gotten a key to her house.

Alex replied that some investigators were going to go through her home to see if they could get any information about how often the killer had been in her house and how he might have obtained a key.

This meant that her house would be considered part of the crime scene and would be off limits for a few days.

Alex offered to provide housing at a safe-house that she might find comfortable for a few days.

She then asked if Yvonne was ready to get checked out of the hospital.

She asked Malia where they would be going to breakfast.

David was the one that answered and said that it was a friend's restaurant that they would be going to that was just a few blocks away.

He took a moment, made a call, and invited someone to join them.

Alex smiled as Malia asked who he had invited, and he replied that he had invited Leilani.

It took Malia only a couple of minutes to arrive at the restaurant.

Alex said that she did not need a menu, but wanted three pancakes with butter between each pancake, sausage, and corn bread.

David said that his friend had what she wanted with a Maui twist that replaced the sausage with spam and the pancake had pieces of Maui pineapple mixed in and the corn bread had a Hawaiian twist as well. The syrup was not maple but was a sweet passion fruit syrup.

Alex smiled and replied that she was very interested in trying out a completely new variation of her maple syrup and plain pancake version.

Leilani walked in and congratulated everyone for having solved the case. She pointed at Alex and said that she had been as skeptical as David had been about solving the case as fast as she did.

She then said that the only thing missing were the bodies.

Alex pointed at Evonne and said that she was the last body, and she was alive and well because they had all worked together to get to the scene to stop the killer.

She went on to say that Evonne's house was going to be locked up as evidence until it could be thoroughly examined, and Alex had invited her to stay at the safehouse.

Leilani agreed that it was the right choice. She asked Evonne how she was feeling and offered to provide counselling services.

Evonne said that she was confused about having been selected as the killer's next victim and yes she would appreciate the counselling service.

Alex asked about Evonne's evening habits and why she had been passed out when Okani went into the house.

Evonne said that she usually had a couple of glasses of wine and watched the evening news and then often watched a movie but went to bed by ten or ten thirty since she needed to go to work. Lately she had found herself still on the couch early in the morning.

Alex looked at Malia and suggested she have the investigators test the wine bottles that were in the house. She added that they should check both the open bottles and the unopened ones.

Evonne commented that she had never been a heavy drinker, but she did have a couple of glasses of wine most evenings.

Alex shared that during her college years she had an incident that caused her to stop drinking altogether and she now focused on tea, coffee, and sparkling water.

Malia said that she was going to try taking up the same habit.

Evonne said that she probably should do something similar, but it would be easier if she had some friends to hang out with some evenings so that she didn't spend so many Friday and Saturday nights by herself.

Alex commented that one could build a support network by giving support.

Leilani then said that she would like to have a local newscaster friend interview Alex, Malia, and David about the case. She hoped by that time to have found the bodies of those in the missing persons list.

Alex suggested that the bodies would be upstream of the cliff in some ravine that seemed to have a lot of stones collapsed into that was likely covered with dead branches.

Leilani shook her head in disbelief, but immediately made a call.

Alex smiled when a few moments later Leilani got a call and uttered the words, "you have got to be kidding."

Leilani looked at Alex and asked how she could possibly have known that the bodies would be in some ravine just upstream from the waterfall and looked exactly like she had described them.

Alex shook her head and said she hadn't known but it made sense that having an easy out of the way body disposal site that was close at hand would be convenient. Putting dead branches and other debris on the stones covering the bodies was how she would have tried to make it look natural.

David commented that Alex had constantly been surprising him and added that knowing how to hunt and what a hockey stick looked like also made it simple to solve a case that no one else had been able to do. He added that he was going to watch some hockey games to see if he could learn anything.

Alex said that he was misquoting her and that she had learned her skill by studying higher math and knew nothing about the game of hockey other than that it had been very popular at her school.

She said she wanted to change her statement to the fact that the data showed an asymptotic curve with a long lead in tail.

Malia smiled and said she preferred the hockey stick analogy.

Leilani then asked the same question the officer at the scene had asked about the shot that Alex had taken. Why the eye?

Alex pointed to Evonne and said she had a choice to shoot her in the back of the head or try for the eye shot of the guy about to slice her throat. She had to make a fast choice of who was going to suffer the ultimate fate and an eye shot of the killer was all she could see; the rest was all Evonne.

Evonne smiled and said that she thought Alex had made a good choice and was glad that she was a good shot.

Alex smiled and said that she was really aiming for the hand holding the knife but got the eye instead and watched as Evonne's eyes opened in amazement.

Evonne looked around the table and asked if Alex was kidding.

Leilani laughed and chimed in that the police target range manager where Alex had taken the Glock to try it out said that he had never seen anyone fire a handgun so rapidly and make only one large hole in the center of the target.

He had sent the target to her, and it was now posted in her office with the word, "I and my detectives will learn to shoot like Alex."

Alex took a bite of her pancake and added a piece of spam and chewed away so she did not have to say anything. When she had swallowed, she simply said, "it's all about practice."

Evonne asked how she could become part of a group of people that seemed to get along so well.

Leilani looked at her and said that she was recruiting for the next police academy class and if Evonne qualified, she could begin training in a month.

Evonne said that she had not graduated with the greatest grades but had a degree from Berkley and other than a speeding ticket in California that she had not paid she had never been in trouble with the law.

Leilani suggested that the traffic ticket get paid and that Evonne come to her office, and they would fill in the police academy entrance application form together.

When breakfast ended, Malia said she was ready to drive back to the safe-house, take shower and get some sleep.

Leilani said that she had to be sure the evidence all got gathered and then she was taking the rest of the day off. She suggested that David and Malia take the following day off and plan a three day weekend after that. They were all going to look good for having solved the case.

Alex asked whether Okina's house had been secured and if so she would like to go there for a walk through before going back to the safehouse.

She also asked if Evonne could be taken to the safehouse.

Leilani said Okani's house was secure, but she had the evidence crew working Evonne's home first.

She called the unit outside of Okina's home to let them know about letting Alex and her detective's in.

Alex thanked her and asked Malia and David if they were ready.

David asked what she was expecting to find.

Alex replied that she was hoping to find trophies.

Malia asked what kind of trophies Alex was thinking she would find.

Alex said that she hoped it was not body parts but other than that she was not sure what she was looking for.

They arrived at the house and were met by the two patrol personnel that were watching the house.

Alex let them know that the three of them were going to check the house to see if they could find any evidence.

David led the way in and once inside asked how they should search the house.

Alex suggested they take a quick look at the downstairs and then start a thorough search beginning from the second floor.

They found nothing from a cursory look of the first floor.

Alex led the way upstairs and began looking in each room. She quickly got the impression that Okina was a very meticulous person and could potentially be labeled a neat freak. He had everything in its place.

There was nothing of interest upstairs.

She now became conscious that if she were to find something she would have to assume the persona of the killer.

He was neat. He was organized. He used a knife on his victims.

Why had he been using such a small knife when she shot him?

Malia commented on how she felt she was walking through a model home that had been prepared to be shown

Alex nodded in agreement and said it was time to look in more detail on the first floor. She said that this time they would need to keep a sharp eye for something out of the ordinary or well hidden.

As they went through each of the rooms on the first floor David asked how confident Alex was that there would be trophies.

Alex replied that she was very confident but was not sure what she was looking for.

In the kitchen Malia again commented on how neat Okina was and the way he had set up his kitchen. She pushed on one of the family of hanging pots and pans. Then she waved her hand across the knives being help by to a board by a magnetic strip down its middle. Finally, she pointed to all the other kitchen utensils on a long board mounted next to the one with the knives.

Alex stopped for a moment as she recalled the scene when she shot Okina. She suddenly felt certain that the trophies would be the knives that he had used to cut his victims throats.

She said that they were looking for a set of knives.

David opened all the cupboards in the kitchen and declared that there were no additional knives anywhere.

Alex led the way into the living room. She looked around and it hit her that the room was not arranged in an optimal arrangement.

It felt as if the room was not laid out correctly.

Why would a neat freak not arrange the living room to a more conventional layout?

She said that what they were looking for was in the room.

She walked over to the reclining chair that faced a large, curved screen on a floor stand and sat down.

The chair was centrally located, and the couch was off to the side.

The room was not organized properly. It was out of balance.

She looked around the room.

Why was the large screen not mounted in front of the painting above it?

She reclined the chair and took in the panoramic painting of a waterfall that stretched across the wall above the television. She recognized it as the waterfall that they had just come from.

She realized that Okani had set up the room so he could relish his time at the waterfall. She noticed that the water fall on the right had a pink hue to it and figure he had edited the picture to show the blood in the water.

She asked Malia and David to see if they could lift the picture off the wall.

David said that the picture was not mounted in the normal way of hanging a picture but mounted on some sort of frame.

Alex looked at the controls on the table to the side of the recliner. One had the name of the television on it. She picked up the other and pressed the on button and watched as the picture went up the wall and exposed a recessed display case below it.

There from left to right with date labels were the knifes that had been used. It seemed that each knife that was used got smaller as time progressed and there was one straight razor in the middle.

Alex knew she had found the trophies she was looking for.

Malia pointed to the memory sticks that were under each knife, and she picked up one memory stick labeled "master."

Alex said she thought those would be videos of the killings and that the one labeled master would be all the individual ones on one memory stick

She asked one of the two to call Leilani and let her know what they had found and that they would leave the picture in the raised position to make sure the folks gathering evidence would have no trouble finding it.

David made the call.

Malia asked if they should turn on the tv and view the memory stick labeled master.

Alex said that she had no desire to view any of the videos. She was sure someone would need to do it, but she was not going to be one of them.

Alex asked Malia to take pictures of the room and a close up of the display of knives. She pointed to the empty knife holder at the far right end and at the name below it.

When David got off the phone she pointed it out to him.

She then quietly told the two of them that on tough days they should remember that they had successfully stopped a very prolific serial killer and saved the life of his last victim.

David thanked her and told her that she had made her mark on his career, and he would be working to up his performance.

He said that he was going to skip lunch and asked to be dropped off at his house so he could get some sleep. He said he would meet them for dinner if they were going to go out.

Alex said that dinner would be the first time she would be ready to get back together, and it was up to the two of them if they wanted to continue the team meals.

Malia replied that she planned to do it until Alex got on her flight to Cincinnati.

9 Maui Resident

*A*lex let the sense of relief flow over her. They had been on time.

They had saved a life.

She let the fact sink in that she had made a tough but correct decision. She had gone back on the horse and ridden at a fast gallop and stayed on for the whole ride.

She had recovered her sense of wellbeing during her two weeks on Maui with Matt.

She had recovered her sense of self confidence in solving a challenging case.

She had saved someone's life and seemingly had put purpose into that person's life.

It seemed that she had improved the work environment of the Maui detectives that had been struggling to work together.

Her purchase of the house, which had become a desire for her to own, was the crowning event of her trip to Maui.

She would return to Cincinnati not the person she was before, but a confident one and the much recovered person that she had become.

Her next session with her analyst would be much easier than previous ones. She planned to continue them into the foreseeable future, and she knew that they would be necessary but confident that she was on much better mental footing than in previous sessions.

She hoped that Trey had experienced a similar renewal in Cancun with Lindsey and Nolan. She wanted him to be back to the man of steel that was her partner. She knew that he too would be a different person. He had suffered from PTSD from his experience in Iraq and then the SLATE case had caused a reoccurrence. He had held himself together much longer than any one she knew.

She knew that all of them would have a lifetime of having to recover from the intense SLATE case, but she knew that each of them would work through it.

They would support each other.

At the restaurant that David had selected to pay off his bet she made a point of ordering Hawaiian crab claws, some purple sweet potatoes, and a pineapple based salad. It was not the most expensive dinner she could have selected but she made the point that she was collecting on her and David's bet about solving the case in a week.

Malia ordered her dinner and thanked David for the bet and her reward.

David said they were both welcome and that losing the bet but saving a life made it easier for him to pay off.

Later that evening, Alex shared that she was going to be a Maui resident and that she would close on the house of her dream before she left the Island. She let them know that she would ask the realtor, who would be handling her property, to schedule a week for each of them but that the week had to be spent there with at least one other person of their choice but not more than six people. The mix of people did not matter.

Alex said that she had found out that the house was not rented and that she was going to have a grill out and then invited them all to have a lunch there on the following day and asked each of them to bring a dish item. She planned to grill ribs, some brats and dogs, some vegetables, and some chicken wings. They should bring the spaghetti, noodles, buttered Italian bread or some food item specific to the islands.

She said that it would be casual, and swimming and snorkeling would be part of the lunch.

Leilani commented that she was very happy that Alex had been able to purchase the house and that she would make sure that the local police came by often to ensure that it was not broken into.

Alex thanked her and shared the fact that the management plan that she was working with the realtor specifically called out daily checks to make sure the property was secure.

Malia asked if she could bring a date.

Alex asked when she had found time to date someone and got a laugh from the three and then said that of course she could. It turned out both Leilani and David also said they would like to bring a date.

Alex said they were all welcome to come with a date and that she felt a little like the match maker in the movie, The Fiddler on the Roof.

A few days later, after she had closed the deal on the house, she turned in her red Jaguar and took the tram from the car rental area to the airport proper.

She checked in and then went to the gate to await the loading of the plane.

She had talked with her parents who were excited to have been able to help her buy a house in Maui. They said they had already talked with the realtor and had scheduled three, three week vacations in the coming two years.

Alex said that she and Matt would be spending two weeks there every year for as far out as she could schedule.

It turned out that everyone in the department sent her a text and let her know that they had already booked their next vacation at her place.

When she got a message from the Angel on the Hill she knew that she was indeed being watched by her southern partner.

Then she got messages from James and Abbie, John and Hanna, and Harold.

Her realtor called and let her know that she had enough folks having made reservations that the property had been scheduled enough that Alex was now making money for the next three years.

Alex felt a sense of relief that her biggest gamble was paying off.

The flight back to Cincinnati was smooth and relaxing.

She was surprised as she got to the baggage pick up area to be overwhelmed by several camera crews and the local news castors asking her questions about the Maui Serial Killer case that she had just help to solve.

She was happy to see Matt towering above the crowd and made her way to where he was standing. After a hug she turned back to the crowd of cameras and began to answer the questions.

She shared that she had worked with some excellent Maui detectives in ending the serial killings. She made the point that the Maui police department and the fire departments had both provided the support that it took to get the killer. She shared the fact that her computer analysis, Johnnie Smith, a Vietnam Veteran, and a magician at parsing data had been key in getting the information that allowed the case to be closed.

When it was apparent that only her bag was still going around on the conveyor, Alex let them know that it was time for her to go home.

The next morning, she went down to Johnnie's apartment with two trays of cookies and muffins that she had just taken out of her oven.

He said that he had to silence his phone because he was getting calls asking for interviews. He pointed at her and said she should not have praised him in public and took the trays from her and said that her cookies were always enough.

She enjoyed his laugh when he welcomed her back from paradise and asked if she wanted a cookie with her morning coffee.

She chose to have one of her blueberry muffins and a cup of his coffee. It was good to be back home.

They rode their bike's in to work and there she got a standing ovation when she went into the bull pen area.

Trevor commented that she seemed to have gotten several inches taller and that her ego must be puffing her up.

Alex smiled and replied that getting him off her back for a few weeks had let her body get back to its normal height.

Bill smiled and said, "touche."

She asked about everyone's vacations and was pleased to hear that every one of them had been able to greatly reduce the tension and stress from the last case.

When Trey walked in, Alex knew just by looking at him and the way he was carrying himself that the vacation in Cancun had been what he had needed.

After a few moments of chatter among them, Alex walked to the Chief's door and knocked. She immediately knew by the look on his face that a new assignment had landed on his desk.

She did not know what it was but simply said that they could handle it.

The End

<u>*Preview of:* **Sins of the Daughter**</u>

<u>*1 Zelda*</u>

*T*here was no moon, the surrounding forest was silent, about a dozen leather covered recliners supported the reposed audience out in the middle of a small clearing in the forest. The black silhouettes of several very tall pines seemed to be poking their tops into the millions of stars overhead. The air was cool, and Zelda's wind break was exactly what she needed to be comfortable. She was impressed by the indigenous young woman, dressed in a traditional tribal outfit standing on the flat bed of the truck that had brought them all out from the hotel to the clearing in the forest.

The young lady introduced herself as Kaseweetin of the Nehiyawak Peoples Nation or also known as the Plains Cree.

She then looked up, raised her arms and in her language seemed to be praying to the stars.

She then introduced her nimosôm or her grandfather that was up on the platform with her.

She said that her, nôhkom, or grandmother had passed away but that her spirit was present, and she was wearing the outfit that her grandmother had dressed in for special occasions. She pointed out the wide necklace and the feather in her hair and added that they had been gifts from her grandmother and mother.

She then added that family life and the social fabric were important to the Cree. She pointed out that her people were no different from so many other societies where family and the interaction with other members of the society were the values that held them together.

She then paused before pointing to a group of stars and described them as the Grand Mother Spider and that just below the grandmother were the seven sisters known as the Pleiades to most civilizations but to her people they are known as Pakone Kisik and surrounded the hole or place where all her peoples came from.

She then paused again and then she shared that the stars held bears, thunderbirds, and more. It held all the spirits of past peoples and animals.

She pointed to the Big Dipper and said that it was known to the Cree as Mista Muskwa or the Big Bear. In the Cree legend, Mista Muskwa was a massive bear that roamed the land doing whatever he wanted. He was a bully who was defeated by the seven brave birds that formed the ring now known as Corona Borealis.

She said that there was also the story of the moose running in circles after being startled. In Cree it is called mooswa acak "moose spirit" because when a moose is startled, it will run in a big, huge circle, and then continue on its way. That is what Mars does periodically in the night sky.

She stopped for a moment and put her hand on her Grandfather's shoulder. She then said that the Cree had The Seven Grandfather Teachings that formed the foundation of the Cree way of life. The seven were Wisdom, Love, Respect, Bravery, Honesty, Humility, and Truth. These teachings were fundamental and were still practiced by the Cree.

She said that the Beaver carried the wisdom, the Eagle that soared so high bestowed the gift of love, the Buffalo not only gave the gift of food and clothing but also the gift of respect, the Bear with all of it many rascally habits gave the gift of courage and bravery, the Wolf was both a symbol of bravery and also of humility and the Turtle with its hard shell and slow, but stead movement carried truth and bestowed it on all. She added that sometimes it gave truth to those needing to finally finish their journey.

She then explained that the Cree were one of the largest native groups in North America and that the name "Cree" came from "Kristineaux," or "Kri" for short, a name bestowed by French fur traders.

She explained that the Cree land stretched all the way across Canada and that the current population of Cree was somewhere around two-hundred thousand and that at one time it had been close to a million but disease, when they first met the white man, had devastated them.

Zelda was startled when a hand lightly shook her shoulders. She realized that she had dozed off. She had yet to check in at her hotel that was in Saskatoon.

The hour ride in the back of the truck back was lost in thought as she once again relived the fight with her sister Aada.

Aada had followed her out to Middle Cove Beach and caught her making out with her boyfriend. The boyfriend had immediately fled, and she ended up physically defending herself as her sister beat her with a tree limb. She rushed her sister and pushed. He sister tripped on a stone and fell backwards. The loud crack had startled her. She had watched as the blood seemed to flow out and spread like a red velvet blanket as it covered the stones on the beach. The evening sun's rays seemed to withdraw and let darkness come across the water and envelop them.

She did not know how long she had stood in silence wondering what to do.

It was hard for her to recall exactly how she had pulled her sister up the hillside to a crevasse where she then dropped her into.

The crevasse was at least ten feed deep.

Once Aada's body was down at the bottom of the crevasse, she had thrown and pushed rocks down to cover her and had collapsed part of the crevasse so that Aada was covered by at least four feet of rock. She took the tree limp that Aada had beaten her with and was able to break loose a large slab of stone that was about ready to fall on its own.

She said a prayer and wished Aada good luck in which ever realm she had gone.

She threw the limb down on top of the stone.

She remembered driving back and parking Aada's car to the student parking lot which was its normal location and then went to her dorm room and fell asleep.

It was several days later before her mother called and asked if she had seen Aada. She answered that she had not seen her for several days. She smiled at the fact that she had told the truth.

But her mother was not satisfied with not knowing where Aada was and Zelda not knowing either.

Aada's death triggered an urge in her mind that defied her attempts to control it. Since Aada's death she had repeated the ending scene on the beach multiple times. In those scenes she surprised her victim with various ending scenarios. The victims were always male. She thought she understood why. Aada's boyfriend had avoided her like she had the plague.

She went out numerous time to the beach as she visualized the killing someone with one of the thousands of stones. Just before her graduation she had gone out and was visualizing and acting out how she planned to kill Dillon when her mother asked if that was how she had killed Aada.

She stopped in shock. Her mother was dressed in one of her best dresses, so Zelda knew that she had followed her for a reason. She smiled and said that yes she had killed her. She asked her mother if she wanted to see where Aada was buried.

He mother just nodded but did not say a word.

Zelda walked slowly up the hill and took her mother up just above where Aada's body was located. She knew that the stones there were all very loose and constantly falling into the ravine. She pointed down into the ravine.

Her mother stepped forward to look.

Zelda gave her mother a slight push and watched as the stones under her feet gave way and she slid down into the ravine with her legs buried in stones up to mid-thigh. She push more stones with her feet and watched the stones get up to her mother's waist.

Her mother cried out and asked if she were crazy.

Zelda nodded and sat down and with the heels of her shoes she pushed with all her might and felt the slab of stone breaking loose and caught a glimpse of her mother raising he arms as if to stop the stone from crushing her.

Zelda remembered laying back and laughing at the stupidity that such an action indicated.

Getting her mother's car and her car back to the City had taken for ever. She would drive one car a few hundred feet and then run back and take that car past the one in front for a few hundred feet. She had done that all night and had finally gotten her car back to the college parking place then had taken her mother's car to the apartment building. A few days later she had packed up all her mother's belongings and put them in her mother's car and had driven the car out and put it to the bottom of a lake.

That day she had been prepared for the hike back to her campus.

She had graduated the following day. She had watched all the kids signal their parents as they walked across the stage. When it was her turn she had smiled and waved just like all the rest.

She had chosen her career based on that urge to duplicate the beach scene. She knew she needed a career that provided the opportunity that would allow her to play out her desire but make it almost impossible to have the act of a missing person be easily connect to her.

She had solved the problem of having a mother she despised for repeatedly making the point of letting her know that she had a name at the end of the alphabet and her sister had one starting with the first letter.

After a few months on the job, she had invited Dillon out for a drink. He was now working as a sales rep for a little company selling fire alarms. She invited him to her room at a motel near where he had settled.

He was still mister, "let me get into your pants." And she did let him, but she took the top. She hit him on the side of the head with one of the beach stones. She took him out to her car and put him in the trunk. She checked out of the apartment. She checked in his apartment and found that he had little in the way of possessions. They all fit in his car and then she drove to the same lake where her mother's car was located and pushed it in. She always wondered how close the two cars sat to each other at the bottom of that lake.

She had had decided that she was going to be number one in as many facets of her life as she could figure out. She was sure that she had reached that position when she buried her last border body.

It was body eighty-two by her count. As far as she could determine every additional body was now going to put her that much farther ahead. And she had many more Canada-US crossings to go.

It had taken three years and three assignment changes. Each assignment moved her ever westward along the border. She was able to maintain a smooth steady planting of bodies at or near each of the border crossings. She had not been in a hurry. She was steady and smooth. She consistently located her victim from a pool of men similar to Dillon.

After making sure they were estranged from family, she planned the timing, the method, and the date carefully so she that everything she did would be seen as "normal."

The move to her third position had taken a little longer than she had wanted but she was in the Great Lakes region and while she waited she decided to take up fishing to kill some time. It turned out she liked fishing after all!

She was currently working on her move to the next assignment that would take her all the way to the West Coast.

A few weeks after her return from her last crossing associated with her current assignment, she was eating lunch in the cafeteria by herself when she overheard two of her co-workers discussing the fact that the department was hiring a detective located in Cincinnati, Ohio, with the reputation of having solved every case that had been assigned to her. The RCMP was asking this detective to help them solve what they thought might be the work of a serial killer.

Alarm bells went off in Zelda's mind. She asked the coworker at the next table, what had made the department ask for the help.

The person that seemed to be in the know replied that the department had a list of missing women and the two bodies that had recently been dug up turned out to be people on that list. She had heard that there were at least twenty women on the missing person's list and the RCMP and the FBI had made no progress in the past year in finding or resolving any of the cases.

Zelda was somewhat relieved that the focus seemed to be on missing young women. That would put the hunters into another area and away from her list of people. She decided that she should do some research on the person whose name she learned was Alex Evercrest. She wondered what made him so special.

She was soon surprised to learn that it was not a male but a female detective. She became concerned as she began reviewing the news reports on this person. One of the reports had highlighted her as "Cincinnati's Black Annie Oakley" and that pushed her over the edge. She decided that she wanted to see this person live.

She was able to use her department's internal computer to get the address where this detective lived.

She researched the Cincinnati area for tourist attractions and learned there was an amusement park, a botanical garden, several museums, an extensive waterfront park, an aquarium, and some great malls for shopping. She decided to take a vacation and check those places out and as a side see this Alex in person.

She had no intension of having any actual contact, but she wanted to observe and get a feel for the person that might be her enemy.

She decided on a bed and breakfast on the Kentucky side of the river that had a view of the Cincinnati skyline. This seemed to be a way to be on location, be comfortable and be outside of the actual city.

Her boss congratulated her on finally taking some time off and using the vacation days she had been accumulating. She urged her to take several weeks and enjoy herself. She asked where Zelda was planning on vacationing.

Zelda had been prepared for the question and she held up two brochures. One for a two-week ship cruise in the Bahamas and one to a resort in Cancun. She did not specify either. It was hard for her to lie but easy to misdirect.

Her boss pointed at the resort brochure and suggested she go there, enjoy the beach, the food, the massages, and the men that frequented the bars.

Zelda nodded and thanked her for helping her make up her mind.

She then went home packed and boarded a flight to Detroit and from there drove to Cincinnati. She felt that by doing so she would not be broadcasting where she had actually gone.

It took her a full day to drive, and she arrived at her rental at the Bluffs of Devou Park late at night.

She ordered breakfast in and spent most of the Saturday morning sitting on the deck enjoying the view. In the afternoon she took a drive into Cincinnati and stopped at the River Front Park and walked along the river.

She saw only a few black individuals, and most were family groups with several people including children. There was one couple walking and holding hands and one sitting in the swinging seats. None of the women were Alex.

Zelda had two photos of Alex in her possession so she felt that she would recognize her if she happened to accidently run into her.

Two riders went past along the pathway on high end touring bikes. She was sure that one was Alex but there was no way to know for sure. It however made her eager to see what Alex looked like in person.

She stopped at the point where she felt she was standing on the spot where the body of the victim of Alex's first case had been located.

She decided to drive to the apartment address she had for Alex and then drive from there to the police station that had been featured in one of the articles and where Alex's office was located. She drove up the street from the park on the street where Alex had been shot by an angry mother and father that blamed her for killing their hoodlum son.

She drove past the apartment building and then went by the public library where Alex had been attacked by a person firing a fifty-caliber machine gun from the back of a pickup and where she had shot and killed the driver of the pickup and the machine gunner and had fired only two bullets.

She scouted out a place where she could see both the front entrance and the side entrance to the police station. It only had street parking and at least on this Saturday the street parking was open.

She did not want to attract attention and decided that Eden Park was her next destination. She parked and walked around the Mirror Lake and stopped at the location where Alex had found the clue that had solved her first case.

She sat down on the wall of the lake and thought about how dangerous a person like Alex might be. She planned to keep close tabs on how Alex approached her involvement with the RCMP. If necessary she would make sure that Alex never made it through the case.

She figured that she would end her Saturday venture at one of the famous local rib restaurants that had an Ohio Riverside view.

The view and the food were both worth the stop. She thought about the rest of her stay and decided that she would continue to develop her understanding of the person she now knew was a true and deadly hunter, and a potential adversary. She had no illusions about how dangerous a person like Alex could be. She had studied Alex's bodily statistics and in bodily terms Alex seemed frail. In action she must be a cyclone of action and destruction. From everything that she had been able to learn, if Alex were keeping score of bodies, she would probably best her own current count and she had faced those that she had killed when they had weapons.

In her case Zelda recognized that she drugged or surprised her victims and then killed them when they were helpless.

A shiver went down her back when she realized that she had just thought of Alex as a number one.

She decided to call it a day but on the way back to her B&B she stopped and bought two bottles of her favorite wine. She planned to relax and think deeply about what might be ahead for her and how she should prepare for it.

She decided that her Sunday would be spent at the amusement park and then she was going to drive out to where Alex had killed three thugs with only the handle of a broken chair. She was really impressed with this person that was referred to as "Cincinnati's Black Annie Oakley." Her initial impression and take was one of admiration. She thought about it for a moment and thought that she should be honest and add that she also had an initial feeling that she should be very afraid of her.

<u>*2 Unnoticed*</u>

*T*he weekend had been a pleasant one. She and Matt had one of their more pleasant weekends. Matt's EMT members had joined them for the first time for a ride from the Ohio river front and on to the Loveland trail. They had started the ride at the River Front Park and biked all the way to Loveland where they had stopped. Alex treated them all to coffee and a muffin at her favorite coffee shop.

The sky was clear, the temperature perfect and there was only a light breeze which would be at their back on the way back. She got to know the team much better, and she got to thank them in a more personal way for having them save her when the angry mother and father had shot her.

The bike ride had been great, but she ended up with a nagging feeling that she was being watched. She kept returning to the beginning of the ride.

As they were taking off, they had gone past the point where the body of the person on her very first case had been found. She was startled to see a woman standing on the edge of the path in the very same spot that she had stood on that early morning, that seemed like only yesterday but had been several years ago.

It sent a shiver up her back, and it reminded her that she had not recently connected with, Samantha, the wife of, Paul Langley, the victim. She put calling her on her to do list.

What bothered her was that as she approached the woman seemed to stare at her and when she looked into her helmet bike mirror she saw the woman staring after her.

She thought of going back but she was with Matt and his team.

She had returned from the bike ride and the thought of the woman came to her again.

Sunday she and Matt went to the park for a picnic and a sat through a concert. They then watched a movie at her apartment and later had a Chinese dinner they had ordered in and then they sat together on the couch and spent the evening reading.

On Monday she and Johnnie followed their normal routine and bicycled in together.

Alex knew that the last several cases had weighed heavily on her and on all of the team. She looked around and watched each of the team members and was relieved to see that they seemed to be well into recovery.

Bill had a cup of coffee and was listening to one of Travis's many tales as they both ate their morning donuts.

Johnnie had biked in with her and was probably the most relaxed of the team. He was a Vietnam veteran that seemed to have nerves of steel. His morning talks and ride in with her had helped her immensely.

She was very aware of her own vulnerabilities but getting regular counseling was of great help. Her very personal and close relationship with Matt put her on solid footing.

The fundamental bed rock that kept her sane was what her parents had always taught her; "Stand on the fundamental principles of honesty, integrity, and treating others the way you wish to be treated." That guidance allowed her to tackle the most extreme cases and come through with only what she considered "flesh wounds," which healed.

The last series of cases had touched her mind, and she had experienced the effects of PTSD and had a new appreciation of what Trey had gone through after his return from Iraq. The counseling and the support they team gave each other made a significant difference.

She was more worried about her partner, Trey, who was a war hardened but who carried his heart on his sleeve. The last few cases had been extremely hard on him.

In one case, he had almost been physically beaten to death, then in the next case his heroics had gotten him so bruised by a shower of bullets hitting his protective gear that the doctor was worried about internal organ damage.

He had a tough exterior and as the doctor noted he also had a tough interior. He had also overcome his PTSD and had coached the rest of the team based on his personal experience.

Alex had suggested that he take several weeks off and go on a real vacation. Today was his first day back from three weeks in Cancun where he had taken Lindsay and Nolan.

Trey walked in with a cup of coffee in one hand and a bear claw roll in his other. He was smiling and was sporting an golden tan. He sat down and asked if she wanted half of the bear claw.

Alex had never seen Trey looking so good and so relaxed. She nodded to indicate she was for half of the bear claw and said that she was looking forward to it, but she needed to go and get a second cup of coffee to go with it. As she walked to the coffee pot, the Chief came to the door to his office and asked her to come to his office after having her coffee and roll.

The look on his face let her know that he was about to assign a case to her and by the looks it was going to be another one of the different cases. She knew that nothing was happening in Cincinnati, so it had to be a request from some other police jurisdiction.

She was aware that each of the recent different cases given the department a significant boost to the budget and the politics were now positive and supportive of "hiring" out their detectives.

Alex decided to take her time and enjoy the bear claw and cup of coffee and not worry about going to the Chief's office.

Johnnie was the first to ask what she thought she was going to hear from the Chief.

Then Travis threw out one of his wild theories that a body had been found in the Himalayas that verified that Big Foot ate humans, and the Tibetans were asking for Alex to come and capture it.

Bill commented that he thought that counseling had been helping Travis, but it was apparent that he was still as crazy as ever.

Trey shook his head and commented that they should check Travis's desk to see where he kept his bottle.

Alex smiled and said it was good to see that everyone was doing well, and she was going to go in and see just what the Chief had that would give them all some purpose other than to exchange meaningless libretti.

Travis called out after her and said he did not know what libretti meant and he didn't have a dictionary.

Alex put up both hands and hunched her shoulder as she walked into the Chief's office.

She could hear Johnnie explain what the word meant as she closed the door.

The Chief asked if she needed anything to drink.

Alex walked over to his coffee pot and refilled her cup and then sat down.

The Chief held up a file and said that the request for help had come from the Royal Canadian Mountain Police or as they were now called, the RCMP, via the FBI. He said that he had gotten a call from their friend Harold Zimmerman of the DEA who had connect him with the FBI Canadian's liaison. He said that Harold had given him warning that the case was unusual in that it seemed to be a case that encompassed most of the Canadian to US border.

The Chief then then described the conversation he had with a Denton Tremaine of the FBI. Denton highlighted that the case had made no progress since the discover of two bodies along the Canadian US border. Now after close to a year of joint investigation of more than twenty cases of missing women they were reaching out to see if they could find a way to break the case.

The Chief looked at her and said that Denton said that he had followed several of her cases and was wondering what it would take to get her assigned to the case they were calling the Canadian Stalker Case.

I told him that money talked but he did not assign the cases and told him that you made the call. I agreed give you the details and he would have to personally talk with the two of us before a decision would be reached.

Alex reached out for the case file and suggested a meeting in Cincinnati. She and the team would prepare for the meeting, and it would be a team decision about taking the case.

She pointed out that she had taken all of what she considered her team through a series of very trying cases and she wanted them to be part of the decision making.

The Chief nodded and agreed that it would be a good idea. He asked what she thought of how each of the team was doing.

Alex replied that it seemed that things were back to normal. Each of them was attending individual sessions with their analyst and they were all still having a group session once a month.

He asked her how she was doing.

Alex replied that her life had also returned to normal, and she had enjoyed the quiet and boring few weeks since her return from Hawaii but was already thinking about when she would be going back to her new home there.

The Chief replied that he had rented a week at her new home in Hawaii. Rose was very excited to go and had said that he should take it easy on her favorite detective.

Alex smiled and told him to tell her that he always took it easy on Trey.

He shook his head and said that he would do nothing of the kind. His home life was good, and he was going to keep it that way.

He gave the file folder to her.

Alex thanked him and let him know that she was taking the team into a huddle room to go over the material together in preparation for meeting with Denton.

As Alex reached her desk, Travis commented that he knew a few big words as well but he did not want to embarrass her so he would just keep them to himself.

Alex held up the file and commented that she had a humdinger of a case that they could swot. But they would need to be able to grasp the basics of construing.

Johnnie started laughing.

Bill shook his head and commented that Travis was causing them all to listen to spoken English that he could not understand.

Trey was also laughing and said he knew the basics of construing.

Travis shook his head put his hands up and said, "I give."

Alex smiled and suggested they all go to a huddle room and review a case that was coming to them from the RCMP via the FBI.

Travis replied that he understood what she had just said except he wondered who the RCMP were. He added that he was now getting bored and missed the noise of gunfire.

Alex led the way to the huddle room and after everyone was seated she pulled out the contents of the envelope. She suggested that she take a picture of each page, one at a time and send it to Johnnie who could post it on the big screen, and they could study the report together.

Bill commented that it would be great because then his partner would be able to understand what the case was about.

Alex ignored the comment and took a picture of the first page and sent it to Johnnie. Once the document was on the screen, Alex pointed out the title.

Trey read the title, "The Canadian Stalker Case." He asked what was being stalked.

Alex sent the picture of the next page to Johnnie. She then sent pictures of all the pages before sitting down.

Johnnie put up the next page which was a summary of what the case was about. It highlighted the possibility that up to twenty-three women were the victims of a serial killer. Two bodies had been found but they were so deteriorated that they had yet to be identified. It seemed that the bodies had been brutally bludgeoned to death. The bodies had only been found because the perpetrator must have been rushed or interrupted while covering the bodies and that some animal had dug them up. The bodies were in remote locations. The Mounted Police had only found them when two different Mounted Police had investigated the areas because of vultures flying overhead.

Alex let out a groan. She shook her head and said that the case was going to be a heart breaker. To solve the case, they were going to have to find many bodies and figure out the pattern the killer was using to find the victims and how often and how he had kept the disappearance of twenty women unnoticeable for the length of time he had.

Trey added that they would most likely be slogging through countless miles of woods trying to find bodies.

Johnnie commented that they should think about using the latest technology and do most of their searching with drones. He added that they could search more territory, and they would go into the woods only when they found some promising sign that needed closer investigation. If they could find some sort of signature or pattern that they could discern from the air they might be able to speed up the discovery of the bodies.

He suggested that they use the two bodies as their base points and first search the miles of space between them. If they found bodies, the distance between them might give them a pattern.

Alex complimented Johnnie for a great idea.

Trevor joked that somebody had been feeding Johnnie too much brain food or maybe if the team fed him more he might solve the case before they all had to face the Canadian biting flies.

Alex laughed and reminded everyone that the last time they had treated Johnnie to a barbeque rib lunch and let him watch logs floating down the Ohio River, he had pretty much solved the case they had been on. All the team had to do was to go in and face crazy gun men trying to kill them.

She pointed to the clock and commented that it was close to lunch time, and she was ready to take Johnnie to watch logs floating down the river.

Trey commented that he was through with the report and wondered if everyone was on board on taking on the case.

Alex countered that they should hold that decision until they met with Denton their FBI contact and got more details about the case and how they would work with the FBI and the RCMP.

Bill seconded her proposal and said that it was too early to close on doing the case. He figured they would, but he was sure there would be some bargaining that they would end up doing before agreeing. He reminded everyone how well the weekend family mini vacations had worked to keep the home fires burning. He was sure that would be one feature he would be wanting the team to repeat. He added that he had no clue what would be available as they searched along the Canadian border, but he was sure that fishing would be one feature that would be available.

Alex agreed and said that she was driving one car. She was going to see if the Chief wanted to join them for lunch. She asked Johnnie which restaurant with a river view he wanted to go to and then asked him to call and make a reservation for six.

She wished that Matt could also be there, but she knew he was on duty. She gave him a call and asked if he wanted to have a carry out lunch for he and his team.

Matt said that he was sure his team would love to get some carryout. He asked if she were paying.

Alex replied that she indeed was, and he and the team could come by and pick up their order when it was ready. She would have the restaurant call them when the pickup was ready.

The Chief said that he would join them for lunch, but he needed to be back to take the call from Denton's boss. He said he wanted to make sure that the financial and authority jurisdiction were clearly defined. He asked if Alex wanted to join him for the call.

Alex shook her head and said she was much more interested in what Johnnie had to say about his take on the case than worry about the money and jurisdiction. She added that the Chief knew where she stood on jurisdiction and investigative control, and she trusted him to make it clear that she did not take orders from any other person but her Chief.

The Chief smiled and said she had taught him well and he had her back.

Alex then led the way out to the parking lot. She let everyone know that the lunch was on her if Johnnie did a good job of sharing his vision of how high tech could help them solve the case and which end of Canada they should begin their search.

Travis commented that Johnnie better come up with a good story because he wanted to be treated to a juicy steak and listen to a tale that he could put his arms around.

Johnnie smiled and said that everyone should order from the top of the menu because he had a crazy tale to tell and a journey, of five-thousand, five-hundred and twenty-five miles, that the team would have to travel to solve the case of the <u>C</u>anadian <u>U</u>nnoticed <u>S</u>erial <u>S</u>talker.

He said that they all should learn to CUSS and laughed at his own joke.

Alex shook her head and commented that she had made a mistake and should have taken him to a burger place so she could save the money for her wedding dowry.

Travis complimented Johnnie on improving the name of the case and he was right at home cussing up a storm.

Bill shook his head and commented that they had not even agreed to take on the case and they had two people that were making jokes about a very serious and chilling one.

Travis shook his head and said it would only be chilling if they didn't get done before the beginning of winter.

Bill pushed Travis out of the door and said he needed to ride with Alex in her old car.

Thank You for reading this far.

To read the rest go to:

https://Remwriter95.net/

About the Author

Ronald E. Mueller
remwriter95@gmail.com

Ron grew up in what is now Flint River State Park in Southeast Iowa. The 170-year-old house Ron lived in is built into a hillside. It faces a 125-foot-high cliff towering over the little Flint River. The house and the land talked to him about; the passing of time, the struggle to conquer the land, the struggles people faced and the wonder of nature.

He climbed the cliffs, crawled into the caves, dove from the swimming rock, collected clams from the bottom of the pond, gigged and skinned frogs for their legs. He trapped muskrats for fur, hunted raccoon in the dead of night, and with only a stick hunted rabbits in the dead of winter.

His young life was outdoors, and nature tested him.

He walked to a one room stone schoolhouse uphill both ways. A stern but warm-hearted teacher, Mrs. Henry was instrumental in shaping his character as she shepherded him from the fourth to the eighth grade.

It was a great way to grow up.

Ron graduated from Burlington, High School, went to Vietnam in the Navy. He graduated from The University of South Florida with an master's degree in engineering, worked for thirty eight years for Procter and Gamble, traveled around the world thirty times.

He has remained happily married for more than fifty years. His daughter and his two sons are all successful and his three grandchildren have all graduated.

His wife has humored and supported him as he became a full time professional story teller.

His experiences inter-twined with snippets of fantasy lend themselves to the adventures he leads the reader through.

Books by Ron Mueller

<u>Fiction Series</u>
The Alex Evercrest Series

The River Front
The Girl on The Grill
Missing
Maggot
Racist
Votive Candles
Windy City
Country Road
Pool of Blood
Sins of the Daughter
Body Parts
The Skull Collector
The Vanishing
The Shadow Fighter
Moonshine
Grief's Trajectory
The Magic Touch
Northern Lights
Alex Evercrest Heroine
Alex Evercrest Collection Two
New Direction
A Family Affair
Disruption
Aftermath
The St. Lebuinnus Church Murder

A Brian O'Neil Novel

Hawaiian Phoenix
Moon Curser
Death Broker

The Problem Solver Series

Solutions
Drug Lords
Border Crosser
The Problem Solver Collection

The Taelo Series
Taelo: The Early Years
Taelo: The Golden Feather
Taelo: Journey of Discovery
Taelo: Dangerous Passage
Taelo: Condor Clan Slingers
Taelo: Circumvention
Taelo: The Journey of Sages
Taelo: Collection
Taelo: Future Leaders Journey

A Taelo Story:
White Swan and Quiet Pheasant
The Child's Name
Floating Cloud
Quiet Rabbit
Busy Bee
Little Otter & Talking Wren
Broken Spear
Burley Bear & Meadow Flower
Taelo Story Collection

Science Fiction

The Savitar Series:
Journey's End
Savitar
Confluence
Savitar Series Collection

Bram Nielson Series
The Fold
The Message
Fold Wormhole
Negative Fold
Ripples in Time
Bram Nielson Collection

Single Science Fiction Books:
Current Past and Future
The Event
The Door
Viajante 7

Published by: Around the World Publishing LLC.

https://www.Remwriter95.net/

www.ingramcontent.com/pod-product-compliance
Lightning Source LLC
Chambersburg PA
CBHW070546100726
47907CB00004B/1286